To Myra,

May all your illusions be happy ones.
It was great to re-connect, let's stay in touch.
Helen

Helen JM
April 19th 2006

THE VILLAGE OF ILLUSIONS

By

Helen Turnbull, Ph. D.

Illustrations by Rob L. Hough

authorHOUSE

1663 LIBERTY DRIVE, SUITE 200
BLOOMINGTON, INDIANA 47403
(800) 839-8640
WWW.AUTHORHOUSE.COM

This book is a work of fiction. People, places, events, and situations are the product of the author's imagination. Any resemblance to actual persons, living or dead, or historical events, is purely coincidental.

© 2005 Helen Turnbull, Ph. D. All Rights Reserved.

No part of this book may be reproduced, stored in a retrieval system, or transmitted by any means without the written permission of the author.

First published by AuthorHouse 11/28/05

ISBN: 1-4208-9158-8 (sc)
ISBN: 1-4208-9159-6 (dj)

Library of Congress Control Number: 2005909222

Printed in the United States of America
Bloomington, Indiana

This book is printed on acid-free paper.

Dedication

To Iraj
You will forever own the place in my heart
that no one else can fill

Acknowledgements

Many people have helped me in this journey. There are too many to mention all of them by name. I would, however, like to thank my niece and my friends who supported me by reading sections of the book as it evolved, providing me with feedback, and enthusiastically encouraging me to continue. Most of all I want to thank Iraj for his unconditional belief in my abilities.

Table of Contents

Dedication v
Acknowledgements vii
Foreword xi
Chapter One 1
   A magical journey 1
Chapter Two 12
   The Nomadic Ms. Cosmopolitan 12
      The Fairground: 15
      The Playground: 23
      The Land of Moderation: 29
Chapter Three 33
   The Village of Illusions 33
Chapter Four 46
   The Lost Brother 46
      The Circus: 46
      The Elephant and the Giraffe: 52
Chapter Five 55
   Queen of Illusions 55
      Bracketing Reality: 56
      Down at the Pond: 59
      Prince Charming: 61
      Reframing reality down at the pond: 64
Chapter Six 67
   Controlling Mr. Fixit 67
      Par for the Course: 67
      Life is a Beach: 70
      A Hole-in-One: 81

- Chapter Seven 85
  - Mrs. Baker's Dilemma 85
    - Facing Reality: 88
    - The State of Anxiety: 93
    - The State of People-Pleasing: 104
    - On the path: 108
    - Connecting the Dots: 109
    - Postscript: 113
- Chapter Eight 115
  - The Happiness Bug 115
    - On a Mission: 115
- Chapter Nine 142
  - Arctic of Ice Valley 142
    - Golden Threads and Silver Needles: 142
- Chapter Ten 167
  - The Island State of Inner Wisdom 167
- Chapter Eleven 178
  - Reflections 178
- The Woman in the Glass 180
- You and Yourself 181
- References 182

Foreword

*The entire universe is a state of mind,
change your mind and change the universe. (Silbey 1987)*

    This book was conceived at the intersection of my perceptions, my memories and my imagination. Listening to my inner voice shed light on the path and allowed me to follow the trail of breadcrumbs.
    It was the summer of 1997; I was sitting on my pool deck feeling quite depressed. I had closed my eyes, partly because I was emotionally exhausted and partly because the sun was in my eyes. When I opened my eyes, a dove was sitting on the roofline of the house, profiled against the sun. The bird flew from the top of the roof to the edge of the lower roof. Given my state of mind at the time, I silently spoke to the dove and asked that if she were a sign of hope perhaps she would fly down and join me. I must admit, in retrospect, that I did not expect that to happen, but much to my surprise, the bird flew off the roof and landed at my side on the edge of the swimming pool. I was speechless. Probably just as well, as I think if I had spoken the bird would have flown away sooner than it did. The bird sat looking at me for a few minutes and then eventually flew back up onto the roofline. I viewed the incident as a sign that things were going to improve.
    On a bright summer evening in May 2003 I was once again on my pool deck when a morning dove appeared beside me, not as close as the first time, but close enough to restimulate my memory of that earlier event.
    The next day I called a friend in the United Kingdom and was bemoaning the slowing economy. She said, "You know, J. K. Rowling was unemployed when she wrote Harry Potter, and she is from Scotland."

I had not realized she was Scottish, so we chatted about that and the conversation ended with my friend saying, "You never know, maybe you should think about writing that book."

Later that afternoon I had been grocery shopping and as I was driving home I started to think about what my friend had said. *Hmm! Me, write a book, a Village of Illusions and States that people live in, like the State of Reality.* As I pulled my car on to the Interstate to drive home, the words *golden threads with anchors on the end* came flowing into my mind and I got goose bumps. It was as if I had become a channel for the information. I knew these were no ordinary thoughts.

At that moment, something caught my peripheral vision on the right side of the car. As I looked over, a morning dove was flying parallel with my car. I cannot describe the feeling other than to say that you might feel the same way if you discovered a pot of gold at the end of a rainbow. When I pulled into my driveway a few minutes later, much to my amazement another morning dove was sitting on the front door step, as if to say, "Just in case my cousin did not convince you, here I am."

The skeptic in me kept resisting. This can't really be happening. As I was preparing dinner, ideas kept popping up and wouldn't quit. There will be a Princess called Amethyst, and the morning dove, of course, will be the national bird of the country. There will be golden threads with anchors on the end and there will be a silver needle with a wise inner eye.

After dinner I sat down at my computer and began to write.

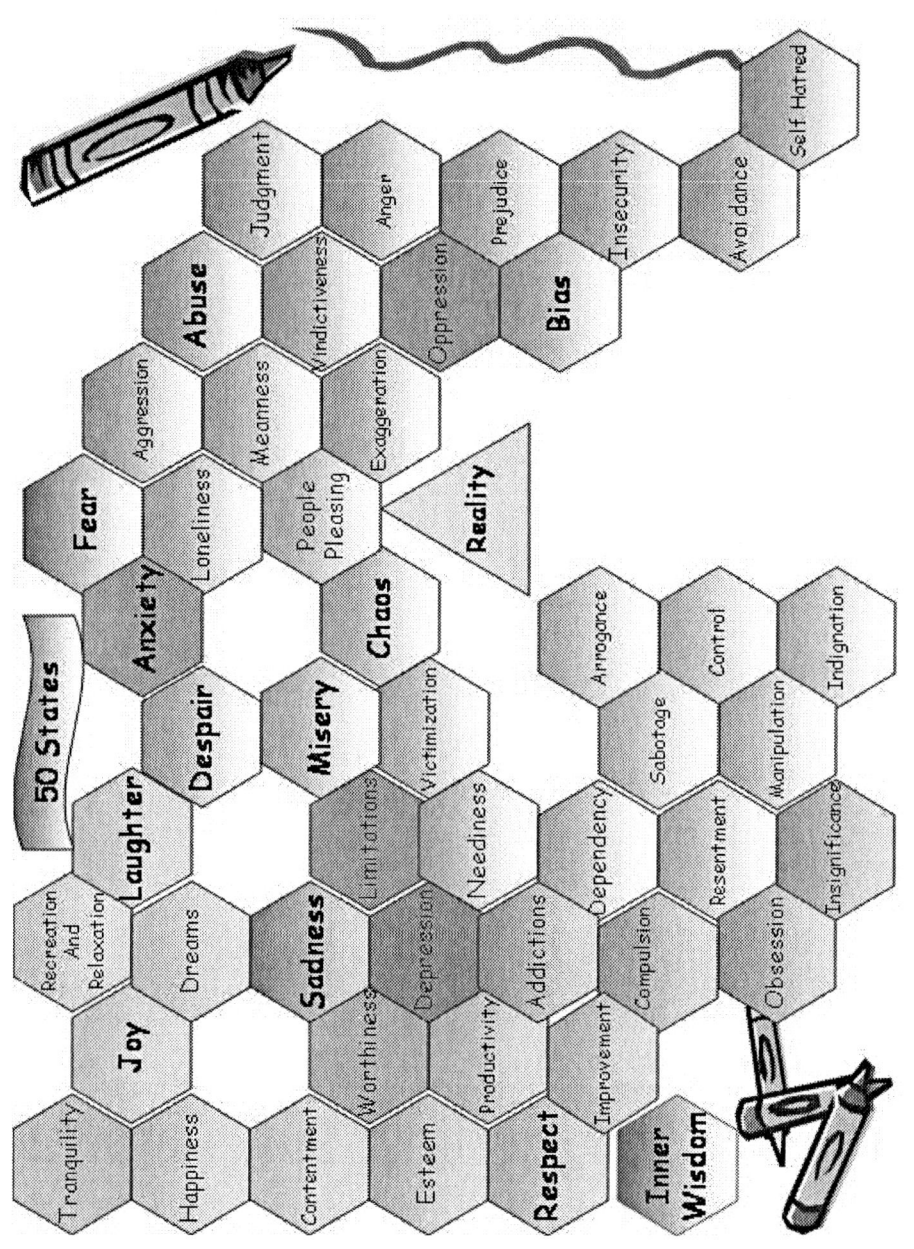

MAP OF EMOTIONAL STATES

Chapter One
A magical journey

Yes, I am wise, but it's wisdom full of pain
Yes, I've paid the price, but look how much I've gained
I am wise, I am invincible, I am woman
Helen Reddy

The phone rang and startled Patience from her daydreaming.
"Hello."
"Hi, Patience. How are you?"
"I'm fine, Serenity. How are you? How are the kids?"
"They're great, thanks. Actually, that is why I am calling. Your niece leaves school this year and the teachers have asked if each member of the family would write her a letter to tell her what they think of her and share their inner wisdom. I was wondering if you would do that for her. I know you are my older sister, but you are young at heart and quite adventurous, so I know she will enjoy your perspective."

"Oh heck, Serenity, you are not serious. Me? You want me to share words of wisdom with my niece. Are you kidding? I am still trying to figure out what I'll be when I grow up! I consider myself to be a bit of a maverick you know."

"I know what you mean. I wouldn't exactly call us mature either, but relative to the next generation I guess we are."

Both sisters laughed at the thought.

"Did you ask Endurance if she'll write you a letter, too?" asked Patience, speaking of their younger sister.

"Yes, she has agreed to do that."

"OK, well I guess I will do it, but you'll have to give me a little time to reflect on what wisdom I want to impart. Guiding the next generation was never on my radar screen and I take what you have asked as a serious responsibility, not to mention an honor and a privilege." said Patience.

"Thanks, Patience, I appreciate that. I need the letter by Friday of next week."

"OK, Serenity, I'll speak to you later this week. Meantime I had best go and put my thinking cap on."

Later that evening Patience was curled up on her favorite seat on the couch. She had had a busy evening, between having dinner with friends and coming home to some paperwork she had promised herself she must complete before bedtime. She was now taking a well-deserved break before heading off to bed. She always needed time to unwind and reflect on the day's events. As her mind began to wander, she found herself thinking about her sister's request earlier that day.

What could she say? What gifts could she impart? It was easy to tell her niece what a wonderful person she was. The difficulty was offering the nuggets of wisdom that would be most helpful.

Patience began to think about her own childhood and the dreams she once had. She remembered that she had always wanted to be a queen or a princess, wearing long, elegant, flowing robes. When she realized that royalty was not an option, she set her sights on becoming a famous ballerina. Her father disheartened her by saying that she was too large to be a ballerina, so she modified her dream yet again and began to hope that she might become a famous ice skater. Sadly, there was no ice rink nearby. She'd had many dreams, many conversations in her head about what she could have become. Accepting less than being a queen, a princess, a ballerina or an ice-skater left her feeling she was settling for second best. Her inner voice never seemed to stop chattering. She had eventually come to terms with the fact that the closest she would get to being a princess would be in her imagination.

It was getting late and this was no time to be making sense of all of these rambling thoughts. She would address the question of the letter tomorrow when she was more clear-headed. As she climbed into bed, it occurred to her that she did not want to disillusion her niece by filling her head with some fairy tale about life. After all, growing up was a serious business and leaving childhood for adulthood had its own pains and rewards. Fantasies were for children, not for grown-ups. Patience had no illusions. She knew she did not live in a "once upon a time" world. She had long since stopped hoping to become a princess and had realized that the idea of finding Prince Charming was just an illusion. Her life to date had not exactly been a fairy tale. She knew that if she dug deeply enough she had a story to tell and life lessons to share. Perhaps she should start listening to all that chatter in her head. It would be like mining for gold, seeking the golden threads that weave the pieces of your life together. All she needed was to find the needle and she could start weaving. With that thought, she drifted off to sleep, slipping quickly into the land of the dreamer.

Patience tossed and turned in her sleep. She normally slept very well and was not used to having a restless night. She tried to find a comfortable resting position, but it was to no avail. She slowly opened her eyes and as she did so, she had a vague recollection of dreaming about a village. She glanced with one eye at the alarm clock on her bedside table and the red neon glared back at her - 1.45 a.m. "Oh heck, I've only been asleep for three hours." Perhaps I should get up and watch some television, she pondered. At that moment there was a noise in the corner of the bedroom and as she peered through the darkness she saw a warm glow of purple and yellow light. She was startled, but for some reason, she was not afraid. She blinked and shook her head vigorously trying to determine if she was still dreaming. The light came into focus and the figure of a woman dressed in soft, flowing, purple and yellow robes appeared at the foot of her bed. Patience sat bolt upright.

"Good evening, Patience. You sent for me?" the soft female voice said.

"Eh? No! Not exactly!" said Patience. "Who are you? And what are you doing in my bedroom?"

"Actually, I am in your dream, Patience. I am Princess Amethyst and I am the guardian of your inner wisdom."

"My inner wisdom! What do you mean I sent for you?" asked an astonished Patience.

"As I recall, you were questioning whether you had any inner wisdom that was worth sharing," said Amethyst. "Perhaps I can help you shed some light on that. Are you willing to come on a journey with me?"

Patience thought for a few seconds, and never being one to shy away from an adventure, quickly said "Oh, why not. Peter Pan was my favorite movie when I was a child. Yes, let's go...but where are we going?"

"To the State of Inner Wisdom, of course," said Amethyst with a gentle smile. She reached towards Patience and said, "Here, take my hand."

Patience, thinking she was not exactly dressed for a trip, asked for a few minutes grace to go and put on some clothes. When she returned, she tentatively placed her hand in Amethyst's palm. She saw a flash of purple light and felt the sensation of being transported, almost as she had imagined "Beam me up, Scotty" would feel. Before she knew it, she found herself standing on an avenue of very large oak trees.

"This place is beautiful. Wow! These trees are awesome. Where are we?" asked Patience.

"Welcome to the Island State of Inner Wisdom, Patience," answered Amethyst. "The oak trees you admire are on Inner Wisdom Avenue, an avenue where I hope you can find answers to your question."

"What question?" asked Patience.

"The one you asked before you went to sleep last night, about not knowing what inner wisdom you had," explained Amethyst.

Before Patience could answer her, Amethyst started walking down the avenue, beckoning for Patience to follow.

Amethyst stopped and sat down on a park bench opposite a very large and majestic oak tree. Patience followed her quietly and slid, almost imperceptibly, on to the bench beside her. Amethyst sat quietly for a few minutes allowing Patience to take in her surroundings. Patience looked up the avenue to the right and saw a very large palace that looked quite grand. In front of her, through the trees she could see a pond with some animals and birds. All together the scene was very pleasant and calming. She was just beginning to wonder what was going to happen next when Amethyst began to speak. "Would you like to look around before we begin?"

"Err. Yes thanks, I think that would be very nice," said Patience graciously.

Amethyst began to walk towards the pond at the bottom of the garden. As Patience stood up to follow her, there was a soft crunching noise under her feet and she looked down to see what she was standing on.

"Oh! The path is made up of oyster shells. They are so crunchy and delicate. They make you want to tiptoe up the path, so that you don't break too many of them," exclaimed Patience.

Amethyst tilted her head to look back at Patience and laughed.

"You might be right, Patience. When people come here I think they do have a tendency to tread carefully, but it is really OK. Just because something seems delicate does not mean that it lacks strength and there is certainly great beauty and strength in an oyster pearl."

"Why do people come here? Do they all come here in their dreams, just like me?" asked Patience.

"No, not all of them. Some people get here just because they are listening to the conversations in their head; some people reach a crossroads where they know that their lives cannot continue the way they are going and are seeking answers and others are lifetime learners who continue to want to expand their sense of self."

"Yikes, Princess, that sounds like very serious stuff. I am not sure I am ready for this," declared Patience in a somewhat agitated tone.

"Patience, you would not be here if you were not ready for this. We are never asked to do something we are not ready for, no matter how difficult or uncomfortable it feels."

Patience had a sinking feeling in her stomach as she realized that seeking her own inner wisdom might be more than she had bargained for. Who really wants to shine a light deep into their soul anyway? Perhaps she could just wake up now and forget all about this dream.

"Come along, Patience, I want to introduce you to some of my friends."

They were walking towards the pond at the bottom of the garden. Patience noticed the beautiful rose bushes on either side of the path and commented to Amethyst that she loved roses. Amethyst nodded in agreement.

"Roses are the embodiment of the human experience. They have delicate and yet complex layers of petals and grow enough thorns to defend themselves."

Patience raised her eyebrows and decided that perhaps she did not want to think too deeply about the roses.

"Oh, look at that!" she said, by way of a distraction.

Amethyst looked in the direction Patience was pointing. There was a rainbow-colored wind chime with a humming bird hanging from an oak tree and a marble tablet with a tribute to the hummingbird.

"What is that about, Amethyst? Let's take a closer look," said Patience as she ran along the path towards the wind chime.

"A hummingbird rings the wind chime every time someone arrives here to recognize that that person is taking the next step in their journey," explained Amethyst.

"And the tribute?" said Patience pointing at the piece of marble in the garden.

"Ah, that is a tribute to the humming bird and to women. I have always been in awe of the qualities that the humming bird possesses. They remind me of the strengths I believe women possess."

Helen Turnbull, Ph. D.

The Humming Bird *

With its boundless energy, endless variety and unique adaptations,
This fearless creature spends its entire life making the nearly
Impossible appear quite effortless.

This, the tiniest and most diverse gem of the avian world, is able to hover,
Fly backward, upward and to the side with breathtaking speed.

Having perfected the technique of feeding its young in mid-flight,
The humming bird is also a study in time management.

Empowered with the spirit of perseverance, the hummingbird has been known
To travel hundreds of miles without a drop of water or food
In order to reach its destination.

Once there, it gently hovers, wings all a-blur, taking sustenance
deep from within the most fragrant blossoms where only it is equipped to reach.

Quite naturally, such activity requires a great deal more energy
than simply gliding through life.

Such ceaseless exertion develops remarkable strength and, ultimately,
the muscle that the hummingbird works hardest, and grows strongest,
is its heart.

(O'Keefe 1990)

The two women walked on in silence, both lost in their own thoughts. The silence was broken by a rustling sound in front of them. Patience looked to see where the noise was coming from.

"Who do we have here?" said a deep bellowing voice.

Patience kept looking and could not see anyone to attach to the voice.

Amethyst smiled and said, "Oh hello, Octogenarian, this is Patience, who has come to spend the evening with us."

Patience was perplexed. It looked as if Amethyst was speaking to the bushes in front of her. Surely they did not have talking bushes in this mystical place. As she continued to stare in the direction Amethyst was looking, she saw a pair of eyes looking back at her and she gradually brought into focus a rather large turtle nestled at the edge of the bushes. A talking turtle no less. Well, at least that was better than a talking bush.

"So! Ms. Patience, eh! What are you hoping to learn this evening?" the turtle said with a professorial plummy upper class accent.

"Yikes, Mr. Turtle, I am not very sure. I know this is my dream, but I kind of don't feel like I am in charge of it," said Patience.

"Ah! You are, you know."

"Then what are my options? What could I learn?" said Patience, not quite believing she was asking these questions of a turtle.

"Well, for starters, you have to be aware of how your behavior affects others. What influences your behavior and blocks your ability to hear?" said a high-pitched voice from somewhere high above her.

Patience spun around to see where this new voice was coming from only to discover two blue jays sitting on a branch overhead. Apparently, there was no limit to the number of talking creatures in this dream.

"Patience, meet Mr. & Mrs. Blue Jay," said Amethyst.

"Nice to meet you, I am sure," said Patience, a little chagrined. She considered herself to be a very good listener and to be self-aware enough to pay attention to how she affected other people.

"Then there is what happened and the story you *tell* about what happened, and they are not always the same," piped up Mrs. Blue Jay. Mrs. Blue Jay was a deep thinker and at times reticent to speak up, but she always enjoyed joining in philosophical discussions.

"What on earth do you mean by that?" exclaimed Patience.

Mrs. Blue Jay flew down to a lower branch to get closer to Patience.

"Well, my dear, quite often we put our own spin on a story and the more we tell it, the more it becomes 'the way it is.' What we don't realize is that that is only our version of the story."

Patience screwed up her face in a contorted way, not really wanting to grasp what Mrs. Blue Jay was saying to her.

"Don't worry, Patience, let's move on for now," beckoned Amethyst.

They continued to walk down towards the pond at the bottom of the garden. Amethyst walked over to a bush that was literally covered with butterflies. Patience was astonished. She had never seen so many butterflies in one place before. She stood quietly as Amethyst seemed to be talking to herself, almost chanting. Suddenly all of the butterflies took off. It looked like an enormous cloud of color as they glided into the air.

"What are you doing?" asked Patience curiously.

"Butterflies represent transformation and remind us that life is in a state of change. I have a butterfly atrium here at the bottom of the garden, and every week I release hundreds of butterflies and send them in the direction of the State of Reality," explained Amethyst.

"What for?" asked an astonished Patience.

"Well, transformation is an important part of the ecology of inner wisdom. It is my hope that when people see a butterfly it stirs their conscience, making them want to look more deeply at what they might want to change about themselves. People can transform themselves, just like a caterpillar breaking free from the cocoon."

"Do you think it works?" asked Patience.

"I believe it does some of the time. Some people will not notice them, others will see them flutter past and just cast a passing glance and then others will be fully conscious. Over the course of a lifetime people can experience many transformations; many inner deaths where a new and evolved self emerges."

Patience fell silent, taking in what Amethyst was saying.

Amethyst waved and turning to Patience said, "Ah, here come Woody and Flapper. I had wondered where they were today."

Patience looked up to see two morning doves gracefully landing on a bush just in front of them.

"Don't tell me, let me guess. They talk also! Right?"

Amethyst raised her eyebrows in a mild look of irritated bemusement.

"What have you been up to today?" Amethyst asked Woody and Flapper.

Woody had lived with Amethyst on the Island State of Inner Wisdom for a long time. He felt very proud because he knew that Amethyst trusted him to work on her special projects.

"Oh, today we were planting seeds with people who spend lots of their time complaining," said Woody.

Flapper jumped into the conversation.

"We are hoping that they will begin to see that other people don't enjoy hearing them complaining and that there is some payoff they get from doing that."

Patience looked mystified.

"Everyone complains at some time and I don't think they do it just to get a payoff," said Patience.

"Oh, sometimes we have patterns of behavior that we slip into and we don't always recognize that these patterns have become counter-productive," explained Amethyst.

"Somehow I think you are all trying to tell me something, preparing me perhaps for whatever else is going to happen this evening," said Patience with a distinctly anxious and questioning tone.

"Come along, Patience, let's walk back towards Inner Wisdom Avenue," said Amethyst.

"What about the Palace, aren't we going to see that?" asked Patience.

"Oh yes, we can do that also. We will take a break later and I will show you the palace."

The two women started to walk, the four birds flew alongside, and Octogenarian headed back towards the pond to join up with his other friends. Soon they returned to the park bench.

"Can I ask you something, Amethyst?"

"Of course, you can ask me anything. This is your dream. Go ahead," said Amethyst.

"Well, I guess I have lots of questions, but let's start with this one. What role do the birds play? They seem to trust you and it is not normal for birds to be so willing to trust humans. That is if you are human! You are, aren't you?" said Patience anxiously.

Amethyst laughed aloud.

"Oh, I am human all right, Patience, it is just that your definition of human may be more limiting than mine. You probably view your boundaries as starting and stopping with your skin and I see your boundaries as limitless. I see the inside as well as the outside. You are much, much more than just your human body. I am the guardian of your inner wisdom. I can help you to see your potential and remove obstacles from your path. However, I can only do that when you are ready to hear me," said Amethyst.

"Does that mean that you co-exist inside my head, like my inner voice? Or do you exist outside of me and kind of fly alongside?" said Patience, feeling like she might be getting out of her depth in this conversation.

"There is more than one way to fly, Patience. I am everywhere and anywhere you care to look for me. The birds are my messengers. When you see a morning dove, it is either there to provide you with a message or on its way to deliver a message to someone else."

Patience fell silent. She thought she knew and understood symbolically what Amethyst was saying to her, but then again, perhaps she was only scratching the surface and she did not want to appear stupid.

"Patience, each oak tree contains a library that holds the stories of people who have overcome obstacles and challenges, people who have examined their lives, asked themselves hard questions and committed themselves to continuous learning. I thought what we could do is visit some of these libraries and perhaps help you to answer your own questions about your inner wisdom. You have a lot more inner wisdom than we can cover in one dream, but let's see what we can achieve this evening."

Patience nodded her head in agreement, not knowing quite what to say. She was not usually at a loss for words, but sensing the magnitude of the moment, she decided to quietly acquiesce and wait to see what magic unfolded.

Amethyst walked towards the oak tree opposite the park bench. For the first time Patience noticed that each tree had an anchor at the base with golden threads attached.

"What's with the anchors?" asked Patience in a flippant tone.

"The anchors represent all the baggage that people drag around with them. The golden threads are not only symbolic of the threads that weave the patterns of your life, but they are also the invisible threads attached to the anchors that are stopping you from achieving your greatest potential. In order to cut the threads you need to be able to see the patterns that are limiting you. You have more control over your life and your emotions than you realize," explained Amethyst in a tone that implied a much more serious answer than Patience was looking for.

Amethyst reached over and pulled the anchor aside, revealing a door leading to the inside of the tree.

OK! This is different, thought Patience. She followed Amethyst to the inside of the oak tree. Inside was an extensive library of beautiful leather-bound books with golden edges. Cherry wood ladders with brass steps led the curious reader to higher shelves.

"Wow! Look at this place. This is incredible," exclaimed Patience.

"Go ahead, browse for a while and find a book that peaks your curiosity," said Amethyst.

Patience proceeded to explore the library shelves and after much consideration, settled on a book tucked away in a corner on the fourth shelf of the library. She handed it to Amethyst, who had been standing patiently waiting.

"*The Village of Illusions.* That is an excellent story, Patience. Good selection. Now let us go outside and prepare for our journey."

"Journey? What journey? I thought you just wanted me to read this book?" Patience said with a mild degree of irritation in her voice.

Amethyst smiled and went outside. Patience did not want to be stuck inside the tree, so she hurriedly followed. Once on the outside, Amethyst raised her hand and Mr. and Mrs. Blue Jay appeared carrying a golden thread with a large silver needle. The blue jays hovered overhead until Amethyst and Patience were seated on the park bench and then they flew over and carefully lay the silver needle in Amethyst's lap.

"What are you going to do with that?" said Patience, somewhat troubled at the size of the needle.

"Relax, Patience," laughed Amethyst. "There is no need to be alarmed. This needle has special magical powers. You have used it to weave the patterns of your life. If we look through the wise inner eye it will take us into the book you have selected and we will be like silent witnesses to the story."

"Oh, you mean sort of like the Wizard of Oz? I liked Dorothy and her friends in the *Wizard of Oz*," said Patience.

"Well, sort of," said Amethyst, slightly bemused by Patience's curiosity and childlike enthusiasm. You picked *The Village of Illusions*. What drew you to *The Village of Illusions*?"

"I'm not sure. I guess I liked the title and just before you woke me, I was dreaming about a village. Anyway, I am curious about illusions and people seeing the world differently, so I kind of resonated with that, I guess."

Amethyst placed the book on her lap and then, inviting Patience to come closer, she placed the silver needle with the wise inner eye over the top of the book.

"Let's take a look and see what unfolds," said Amethyst.

Patience was aware of feeling quite tentative, but her anxiety melted away as she looked through the eye of the needle and felt herself drawn into the story.

Chapter Two
The Nomadic Ms. Cosmopolitan

*Experience is not what happens to you; it is what
you do with what happens to you.
Aldous Huxley (Photiou 2001)*

"This is Reality Airlines announcing the departure of Flight Number 56 to Anywhere," the loud speaker boomed out anonymously.

Ms. Cosmopolitan was anxiously waiting to board. She had an important meeting to attend in the town of Anywhere and she was looking forward to arriving there. She always liked to board the plane first as she knew that if she managed to get on board early, she could safely put her luggage in the overhead bin without fighting for space with the other passengers. She was a frequent traveler and comfortably maneuvered herself through airports, airlines, trains and hotels. People who occasionally traveled with her used to express amazement at the speed and elegance with which she negotiated her way to her destination. One of her friends had jokingly put another perspective on her navigational skills in airports stating that she "moved so fast she knocked over old ladies in her wake and didn't even notice." She traveled through life in style, always staying at the best hotels, riding in limousines and eating at the best restaurants. Berry Cosmopolitan was someone whom others described as having "presence and charisma." When she walked into a room, people knew she was there.

Today, however, Berry was not feeling full of presence and charisma; she was feeling agitated as she boarded her flight and she could not figure out why.

In the meantime, back at the village, it was another warm sunny day and Veronica was feeling quite happy with herself. She was getting ready to go and meet her friends. They were playing tennis and she had agreed to meet them for lunch. What a nice life she had! She felt lucky to have such a beautiful home and to live so close to Friendship Golf and Tennis Club. The phone rang just as she was about to leave. Veronica felt harried, as she was already running late, but never one to miss a phone call, she felt compelled to answer it.

"Hi, Veronica, it's Carmaletta. I was wondering if you are going to the luncheon on Wednesday?"

"I am not sure, Carmaletta. I'm trying to lose weight and if I go to the luncheon I will most probably end up eating all the wrong things. It's OK for you. You never have to worry about losing weight, but I do. I wish I were as skinny as you are," exclaimed Veronica with a deep sigh.

"Oh, come on, Veronica. First, you know that I am trying to lose weight also. I have gained five pounds you know and it's all relative. Five pounds on me is a lot. Anyway, it will be fun, please say you will come. Veronica sighed. "All right, Carmaletta, if you insist. I must rush, I am running late today."

"OK, see you Wednesday then, I will sign us both up," said Carmaletta.

Veronica was very unhappy being overweight and it caused her to lack confidence. Every day she told herself she would do better and every night she would go to bed chastising herself for having failed again. She worried constantly about what other people thought about her. Recently a friend invited her to go to the beach for the day and she declined, making an excuse about being busy. The truth was she was too embarrassed to wear a swimsuit. What had happened to that slim young woman she used to be? Most days she felt so defeated she would find herself heading for the refrigerator for more comfort food.

Carmaletta Spatts, on the other hand, had no obesity problem. Quite the contrary, she was a tall, angular woman. She was attractive in a fashion magazine kind of way. On the surface, she was friendly with people, but in reality, she was quite judgmental and moody. Her friends were not sure what to make of it. People wanted to be friends with her, but quite often, they were not sure what she was going to say or do. If she decided that she was upset at you, she would say unkind things and then just drop you, albeit temporarily.

Across town, Jasmine was busy getting herself ready to face another day at work. She asked her husband repeatedly, "What do you think my new boss will think of me? Do you think he will like me? What if he doesn't?"

Helen Turnbull, Ph. D.

Hugh had been spending the morning trying to reassure her that everything would be fine, but he was getting tired, knowing that Jasmine was not listening anyway. She seemed to live in the State of Anxiety and was always worrying about what other people thought of her.

What does it matter anyway? Hugh thought.

On the way to work Jasmine often met up with her friend Rose. Rose and Jasmine really liked each other. Rose was a very gregarious person, kind and accommodating. Other people could influence her easily and she was always doing what they asked, sometimes when she did not even want to. She was also emotional and got her feelings hurt very easily. She always seemed to have some story or another about how other people were deliberately doing things to hurt or displease her. As much as Jasmine loved her, she sometimes wished she would stop worrying so much about others' opinions and just live her own life. Jasmine laughed to herself as soon as she had that thought about Rose. How funny, she thought. Hugh just said the same thing about me this morning. Perhaps Rose and I are more alike than I realized.

As they were walking to work they bumped into Carmaletta.

"Hi, where are you off to today?" asked Jasmine.

"Oh, I am just going to do a little shopping and then I am off to play bridge with some friends. Are you going to the luncheon at the Club next week? I was just talking to Veronica and she said she would go. Mind you, I had to work hard to persuade her. She is always complaining about dieting. I never met anyone who talked so much about dieting and never lost weight. What a joke," said Carmaletta.

Jasmine and Rose rolled their eyes and laughed. They did not really like the fact that Carmaletta was being unkind about Veronica's attempts to diet, but they had to admit that Carmaletta was right. Veronica had tried every diet known to man and had never lost more than five pounds, which she always gained back quickly.

"Yes, we will be at the luncheon. We will see you there. Must rush or we will be late for work," said Rose, anxious to limit the gossip about Veronica.

"Please fasten your seat belts. The captain is beginning her descent into Anywhere. We will be on the ground in 10 minutes," the flight attendant announced.

Ms. Cosmopolitan looked up from her book for the first time since the flight departed. She liked reading on the plane, as it helped pass the time. She could lose herself inside the pages. The book she had been reading, which she had purchased that morning at the airport, was called *Self*

Illusions and she found herself thinking about that as the plane landed. What illusions did she have about herself?

As she walked through the airport, her cell phone rang. The voice on the other end announced that her meeting for the day had been cancelled.

"You're joking!" she exclaimed. Apparently not. They were dreadfully sorry they told her. They had hoped to catch her before she left Illusions. A last minute emergency had cancelled her meeting.

Ms. Cosmopolitan now found herself having to spend an idle day in the town of Anywhere with nowhere particular to go. She could catch a flight home later that evening, but not any sooner.

The Fairground:

It was a nice day so Berry Cosmopolitan decided she would go for a walk and then perhaps she would have lunch and do a little shopping. Berry had learned long ago that there is no point in fighting something you cannot change, so accepting her fate, she pragmatically decided to make the best of the day. As she walked through the park, she noticed the morning doves pecking at the ground and a little boy throwing pieces of bread to them. She had heard that morning doves like to eat small stones to assist with their digestion. She wondered if humans would be more grounded if they ate small stones. She laughed at the thought. She walked on and eventually came across a fairground. The annual fair must be in town, she thought. What fun, I have not been to a fair in years; I think I will spend some time there. As she walked into the fairground, a butterfly imperceptibly fluttered past her.

She visited all of the sideshows, throwing ping-pong balls into bowls with goldfish in them. (To be accurate, NOT getting ping-pong balls into bowls with goldfish in them). At another sideshow, she actually won a small soft toy by tossing three balls into the same clown's mouth. Quite an accomplishment, she thought. It may prove to be her major achievement for the day. She spotted the Ghost Train and decided she was going for a ride. It always scared her but made her laugh at the same time. The fear tactic illusions inside were preposterously obvious and yet at the same time it held an allure from her childhood, from the days when her father used to take her and her brother and her on the Ghost Train.

She did not much like the rollercoasters, so she avoided them and eventually she came to the Hall of Magic Mirrors. She thought the mirrors were probably a little corny. Why would you want to see yourself looking in worse shape than you already are? she pondered. Despite her reservations however, she found herself wandering towards the ticket booth, paying her money and proceeding in.

Helen Turnbull, Ph. D.

FAIRGROUND SCENE

THE VILLAGE OF ILLUSIONS

As she walked towards the first mirror, she had a strong sense of being there alone. She hesitated. Maybe I do not want to be wandering in here on my own, she thought. Perhaps I should back out now. However, something compelled her to keep moving forward. As she approached the first mirror, she saw her shape changing. She laughed, having become small, thin, and distorted around the edges. She thought she would like to be thinner, but not with this look. As she was blinking and trying to take in what she was seeing, the figure in front of her began to focus more clearly and she thought she saw her friend, Jasmine. Just as she had that thought, she found herself swept inside the mirror and the next thing she knew she was standing beside Jasmine.

"Oh, hello, Berry," said Jasmine somewhat coolly. "What are you doing here? I thought you did not like me anymore. I thought you were angry at me."

"What am *I* doing here?" she stammered, with, uncertainty and anxiety in her voice.

Berry thought of herself rather formally and normally preferred strangers to use her full title, Ms. Cosmopolitan, but Jasmine was her friend. Well, she thought she was. Berry looked at Jasmine strangely and said, "What are you talking about? Where are we?"

Jasmine did not answer her, but instead invited Berry to come for a walk with her. Berry looked back to see if there was a road out of the mirror, but as she could not see anywhere to go except forward, she decided she had no option but to comply. They walked down a path that had beautiful flowers and bushes on either side. Eventually they came to a small cottage, which looked very inviting. There were a number of stone steps surrounded by flowers, including gladioli, passionflowers and sweet peas. There was a veritable outburst of colors and a sense of spring in the air. These flowers specifically promoted friendships, but Jasmine and Berry did not know that. The steps led up to the door of a stone cottage. They looked tentatively at each other and then Jasmine knocked on the door. A voice from inside shouted for them to come in.

Sitting in the corner in a rocking chair was an old woman. Berry thought she looked like Old Mother Hubbard from the nursery rhymes she remembered as a child. Something about "living in a shoe and having so many children, she did not know what to do." This house did not look big enough for lots of children and she was definitely not living in a shoe. No, she was getting her nursery rhymes mixed up; it was the old woman who lived in the shoe that didn't know what to do. At that moment, Berry did not quite know what to do, either. At that moment, Berry did not quite know what to do, either.

The old woman turned to them and said, "Come in, children, have a seat. Allow me to introduce myself. I am Mrs. Reflection, Emma Reflection, but everyone calls me Ma, so you may do the same. Would you like a cup of tea?"

Berry was quite startled at the thought of being called a child, but no matter, she did like the sound of the tea. Now who should be there serving tea, but Rose? Rose, of course, was all smiles and being very helpful to everyone, with a look on her face that said, "Aren't I good, doing this for you; you do appreciate me, don't you?"

By this time, Berry had temporarily given up control, ceased to be amazed and was telling herself that she was willing to let the process unfold. What next? she wondered.

"So what is happening in your lives?" the old woman asked as tea was being poured. "Tell me about yourselves."

Jasmine spoke first. "Oh, lots of things are happening in my life," she said eagerly. "I have a new boss and I am worried about whether he will like me. I am worried I might lose my job and then we would not be able to pay all the bills. I am learning to play tennis, I am not very good at it, and I think the other women are impatient with my incompetence and I am worried that they talk about me behind my back, and also maybe they don't want me there. My son has a job now away from home and I worry about whether he is eating three square meals a day. My husband is wonderful, but he gets tired of my worrying all the time. He calls me a worry wart." She laughed at the image of herself. "Oh, and one more thing, I'm worried because I think I have upset Berry and I am not sure why."

Jasmine fully expected an appreciative response from Ma Reflection and waited with anticipation. Instead, Ma smiled, turned to Berry and said, "And what about you? What is happening for you?"

Berry, always keeping her defenses up, considered her response very carefully. "Life is going pretty well really. I've had my ups and downs over the years, but for now I feel pretty good," she replied in a guarded tone.

"Oh, that is good, my dear," replied Ma. "Tell me about the important people in your life."

What an odd and somewhat intrusive question, thought Berry. Nevertheless, she felt strangely compelled to answer it.

"Well, there is my husband, Crandon, my mother and two sisters, my brother, whom I don't have much contact with, and my many friends."

"What about Jasmine? Is she your friend?"

"Yeaaas!" said Berry, hesitating over the word.

"You had to think about that, Berry. What is that about?" asked Mrs. Reflection.

"Well, no, she is my friend," said Berry, recovering quickly and not realizing she was being so transparent. "It's just that she upset me recently and I don't always find it easy to get over that. Sometimes I wish I did."

"See, I knew I was right," said Jasmine jumping up and down.

Rose, who was always trying to keep the peace, was looking at her with a grimace on her face that said, "Oh please, Jasmine, I don't want you to be hurt. Don't think like that."

Ma Reflection indicated with her hand for Jasmine and Rose to calm down and said to Berry, "How do you think the people in your life view you?"

All three friends were very surprised. That was not where they thought this conversation was going.

Berry feigned surprise and miscomprehension. "I am sorry, ma'am, but I'm not clear what you are asking us."

Ma smiled patiently and said, "If I were to ask your friends, what personality traits would they attribute to you?"

"I think they would say I was kind, intelligent, generous, warm-hearted, and sociable, had good values and high integrity, successful in my professional life, generous to my family and a good friend. Oh, and a pretty good tennis player," she added with a laugh.

"And what about the negatives, Berry? What do you think people don't like about you?" asked the grandmotherly figure.

Berry was very surprised. Negatives? Why should she talk about that, particularly in front of her friends and a complete stranger?

Jasmine and Rose lowered their eyes, sensing Berry's discomfort, but at the same time were curious as to what she would say. A silence fell over the group as the old woman waited patiently for Berry to answer.

After a few minutes, Berry began to speak. "I think they might say that I have a very strong personality and that I am used to getting life my OWN way. I can be quite domineering and controlling and I often take over the conversation. I have a very good control of language and speak very assertively, which is not necessarily a negative, but it can intimidate other people. I am very self-centered and am usually most happy when the conversation is about me. Is that what you meant by negatives?"

"Whatever is true for you will work, I think," said Ma philosophically.

"And you, Jasmine, what about you?" asked Ma. "What would you add to that about yourself?"

Jasmine loved talking about herself, so she was thrilled to be invited to do so.

"They would say I am a very kind person, not as bright as Berry, but I am not stupid either. I would do anything to help people; I am a good mother and wife. They would also say that I am very insecure and that I am a big worrier. I do not like to be in the sun as it is too hot for me and I do not eat enough. I am a very fussy eater, you know. Many things are not good for me. I am allergic to them. People just do not understand that I cannot eat all the things they want me to. I can't eat ...."

"OK, Jasmine, thanks," said Ma Reflection, stopping her before she launched into a full description of her limited menu habits.

"Oh, don't you want to know about my negatives also?" asked Jasmine.

"I thought those were your negatives, Jasmine," said Ma Reflection with a laugh.

Jasmine continued, seemingly happier to outline her faults than her positive traits. "I am a very insecure person, you know. I know that I am too tentative and not at all a risk-taker. I think I hold my husband back as he has always wanted to do things that are more exciting and I feel too scared to try, or to let him try. I think almost everyone is brighter than I am, even though I know that I am not stupid. I am a bit of a wallflower, really, and am not a big talker. I have many small idiosyncrasies, which I am sure drive other people to distraction. I have health problems and therefore, I have become quite concerned about lots of things.

"That is a long enough list, Jasmine. Maybe you should stop now," said Ma with a kind smile.

"And you, Rose, what would you add?"

Rose smiled demurely and lowered her eyes. "They would say that I was also kind and helpful and that I am always there for them. As for negatives, you should ask my husband. He says I am too easily influenced by other people, including him. He thinks he is the exception. He says I am always changing my mind and doing things I do not really want to be doing. Too accommodating, he calls me." She became quiet and thoughtful for a moment.

"Oh, and another thing, I get my feelings hurt very easily. I take things very personally. When I decide someone has hurt me I do not like to be with him or her for fear of being hurt again. People say I talk too much. They are not as kind as you think they are, people, I mean, and sometimes I just sit down and have a good cry. My grandmother, God rest her soul, she was like that, too, when she was alive. I guess I take after her."

Ma Reflection leaned back in her chair, put her hand on her chin and looked at them all pensively for what seemed like a very long time. They waited in silence, feeling as if somehow they were in court awaiting a verdict.

Eventually she spoke.

"So what do you make of all that? How do you reconcile what others think of you and what you think of yourselves? It requires a little reflection, I think."

Berry, who was secretly glad that she had maintained her own counsel and not disclosed as much as Jasmine and Rose, tried to be smart and said, "Well, actually we would be interested in what YOU think."

Ma smiled a knowing smile and looked over at Rose who, after all, had admitted to being much more accommodating.

"Well, it is a funny thing, but when I was listening to the other two stories I was agreeing with them," said Rose. "I was not only agreeing with their descriptions of themselves, I was thinking that I had some of the same characteristics, good and bad."

"Yes," said Jasmine as if she had discovered gold, "I know what you mean. It was as if you were both telling my story, too. I recognized parts of myself in your story and I can see how you would see parts of yourself in my story. The good and the bad parts, actually."

Berry sat straight up in her seat. Now this had her attention. "What? Are you saying we are more alike than we are different?" she said, aghast at the thought.

"Yes," Ma Reflection said, "I do believe you are." Before Berry could even answer her, she went on to say, "If the descriptions you just heard were about one person and not three, and that one person was YOU, would you accept what people think of you? Do you believe what they ascribed to you? Is it valid?"

The room fell silent. The three friends sat and thought about the significance of that question for a very long time. Ma picked up her knitting from the side of her chair and began to knit, waiting for them to consider her question. She was knitting a large quilt with golden colored wool and it looked as if she was knitting the same pattern repeatedly.

It was Rose who spoke first. "I would say that all of it is true. I am working on being less emotional. I know I get too easily hurt and I am trying to be tougher. I am always giving toxic people too much power over me. But I would really prefer that you did not say unkind things!" she said with raised eyebrows and one of these looks that said, "Is that OK with you?"

Jasmine added, "Yes, I would accept most of their observations, even if I don't like some of them. I am trying to worry less, but it is not easy. How do I do that when I have so many worries? Just look at the mess we are in here, for example. How did we get here?" She stopped what she was saying, realizing that she was worrying again. Everyone laughed.

Berry was once again last to speak and everyone waited. Berry had more to say. She leaned forward, put on her most serious look and said, "If I am to accept that what all three of us have presented is also part of me, then I feel that I must add some pieces of me that perhaps I have held back until now. I feel I have not been totally open with you." Jasmine gasped, Rose grimaced and Ma smiled a knowing smile.

Berry continued, "When I answered your questions earlier I was feeling defensive so I did not share with you what I thought people thought of me." She cleared her throat and sat straight up in her chair.

"I agree with all of the things that Rose and Jasmine said previously, not only about themselves, but also from the perspective that it describes me, too. I would add, however, that in addition to being warm, friendly, sincere and open, I think my family and friends might also tell you that I can be self-centered, demanding, intolerant and judgmental. The positive side of these qualities, such as knowing what you want and getting it are helpful qualities in getting through life, especially when you travel alone as much as I do, but just like anything in life, when used to extreme they become negatives. I do not like myself when I am living in these negative moments. Recently I have been trying very hard to catch myself and change directions."

A silence fell over the room. Everyone was lost in her own version of Berry's thoughts.

After a few minutes, Ma Reflection offered them some more tea and told them that she thought they had made a good beginning to realizing how connected we all are.

"Just remember, girls, the good you see in others is usually reflective of the good in you and conversely, the negatives you see in others are usually negatives you possess, actively or passively." She concluded the afternoon tea session, adding, "It has been lovely seeing you. I do hope that you have gained some insights from our visit together. I have enjoyed meeting you and sharing tea together. I have some other people to meet today so I really must be getting along."

It felt like a somewhat abrupt ending to a surprising tea party, but then again, everything about this trip was beginning to feel surreal. Just as they were leaving, Ma called out, "Oh by the way, Berry, what were you angry at Jasmine for?"

"Whatever it was, I don't remember and I feel certain it was not worth losing our friendship over. I think I am learning that I need to cut my friends and myself a lot more slack. Perhaps not take myself so seriously," replied Berry, much to Jasmine's delight.

Emma Reflection had spent all of her life living near mirrors. One thing she was certain of was that what one person saw in her own life mirror was merely her own construction of reality and that when other people looked at the same picture, they saw something different. Mirrors and reflections were interesting things. You could see the good, the bad and the ugly sides of yourself depending on the angle you were viewing and if you were very skilled, you could learn to be open to seeing the parts that other people could see. Reflections are what it is all about, thought Emma as she watched the three friends disappear from view.

The three friends found themselves outside the cottage, walking back towards the mirror. They hugged each other and agreed that this had been a very profound experience.

"Let's remember all the good characteristics we have and not just concentrate on our shortcomings," one of them suggested. "It seems we all have our fair share of both." They laughed and all agreed, vowing to be more patient with each other in the future.

As they walked towards the mirror, Berry saw something floating to the ground. "What is that?" she said. She bent down to pick it up and it was a label. It read "judgmental."

"Oh, look," exclaimed Berry, "one of my labels has just fallen off. Should I put it back on?" They all laughed.

As if it had all been a dream, Berry found herself on the outside of the mirror. She stood for a minute trying to catch her breath, realizing as she did so that she had a choice to make. Go forward and face another mirror or turn and walk away.

The Playground:

For a moment, Berry contemplated leaving and not getting her money's worth. This was definitely more than she bargained for. On the other hand, she thought, in for a penny, in for a pound. It was scary contemplating the prospect of exploring other parts of herself. Never being one to shirk life's opportunities, however, she stepped forward. This time the image in the mirror was not so kind to her. It made her look much heavier than she actually was, grotesque in fact. Maybe not, she thought, turning away. It was too late, the mirror's energy field had grabbed her and she found herself sliding down a very fast slide with rapid twists and turns. It was quite an exhilarating ride. When she landed at the bottom, she had half expected it to be a water slide and was preparing to swim, or at least get wet. Instead, she found herself sitting waist deep in some kind of sticky stuff. Yuck! What is this? She thought.

Over in the distance, she heard noises and as she tried to gather herself she heard, "Jack Spratt could eat no fat, his wife could eat no lean, and so, between them both you see, they licked their platter clean." (www.rhymes.org.uk 2003)

When she finally extracted herself from the thick liquid, she realized that she was back in her childhood and was no longer her adult self. She walked over to where the noise was coming from and saw that it was her old school playground. Groups of children were playing together. Two of the children looked like Veronica and Carmaletta.

TOFFEE POND

"Oh, Berry, you fell in the toffee pond. What did you do that for?" Veronica asked with a worried look on her face.

"Perfectly gross!" shrieked Carmaletta. "Dr. Gilmore is going to be angry at you. He will send you home. He will tell your mother. You know we are not supposed to go near that Toffee Pond without permission."

Dr. Gilmore was the school Principal and he was indeed a fearsome creature. His office was in the middle of a long curved sweeping hallway that had glass windows overlooking the playground. He wore a long black robe and had a long pointed nose and it seemed that he could always smell trouble. All of the children were afraid of him as he ruled the school with an iron fist, or more accurately an iron nose. When he spotted trouble or was angry about something the children could see him coming. He would swoop out of his office and walk so fast through the curved hallway that his nose seemed miles ahead of his body and his cloak was billowing like a tent behind him. Thankfully for Berry, today he was nowhere to be seen.

"C'mon, I have spare clothes in my locker. Let's get you cleaned up," Veronica said.

Carmaletta looked on with disdain and wandered off to be with some more sophisticated children. Carmaletta Spatts did not get her name for nothing. She was known for having small spats with the other children. She could be very friendly and then suddenly she would say something that would make you think she should wipe the frost off her tongue before she spoke, or at the very least engage the sensitive side of her brain. She used to say things to hurt Berry, which were usually about Berry being fat, and Berry would go home and tell her mother. "She must be quite unhappy at home to be so unkind. Don't worry, dear," her mother would tell her in a consoling voice. Berry did worry and quite often had her feelings hurt by Carmaletta. Despite that, Berry did care for Carmaletta. Sometimes she would defend her when the other kids were angry with her, although there were days when even Berry had to admit that Carmaletta's behavior was indefensible.

Veronica, Carmaletta and Berry had been school friends for many years. It was a funny thing having two best girlfriends. Sometimes you were friends with them both at the same time, sometimes you were only friends with one and the "chosen" one would switch around. It was never clear to Berry what caused her to be ostracized, or indeed what it was that would cause her to be friends with Carmaletta at Veronica's expense or vice versa, she just knew it would happen. The good news was that it never lasted long.

She liked things best, however, when they were all friends.

After school, the three friends went off to their favorite coffee bar. This was the "in place" to be. The coffee bar was quite a small restaurant with a coffee shop upstairs and a narrow winding staircase leading down to the basement. The children called it The Cave. They used to buy themselves an iced coffee and then go down to The Cave and listen to music.

"I'm hungry," said Berry.

"So am I," said Veronica. "Let's go upstairs and get something to eat."

"Oh, you two are always thinking about food," said Carmaletta with a look of implied disapproval.

Berry and Veronica ordered a hamburger and fries, followed by an ice cream sundae. Carmaletta, on the other hand, only ordered a salad with some grilled chicken, at which she carefully picked around the edges. She was not EVER going to become as overweight as her two friends.

Truthfully, while they were her friends she did not like the fact that they were both overweight. While they obsessed about eating food, she was obsessively careful about what she ate. Perhaps too careful?

The road leading back to the school was an interesting one. The children had to walk past a lovely church, which they could see through the iron fence, and then they came to a large hedge. If they stood on their tiptoes, they could see into what looked like a garden, but was actually a Bowling Club where people played lawn bowling. In the summer, it was fun to watch the bowling, so long as you did not forget the time and make yourself late for school.

A little further on there was a turn in the lane and you found yourself on a very narrow bridge covered with foliage from the trees in the woods below. It was only minutes from the school playground. Some days it seemed like a very friendly bridge, with lots of sunshine and foliage and others days it was quite dark and sinister, especially on dull cloudy days. Berry never liked finding herself on the bridge alone. Sometimes after school, her younger brother would go off to play with his friends and he would go down to the woods below. On these occasions, Berry would have to go and find him. She hated doing that and was always nervous of the bridge on those days. Today as she crossed the bridge, however, it was a bright sunny day. She had gotten ahead of Veronica and Carmaletta and she was rushing, as she knew they were at risk of being late. Dr. Gilmore did not like you to be late and if he caught you, he would demand that you come to his office and he would give you an enormous lecture the size of his nose about discipline and timekeeping.

Suddenly, right in front of her, and much to her astonishment, a large panda bear dropped out of a tree.

"Hello, Berry," he said with a friendly voice. "I know you are rushing, but I was kind of hoping you would come and play with me for a little while."

"Oh, but I will be late and Dr. Gilmore...." Berry started to protest, wondering at the same time why she was having a conversation with a panda.

"Don't worry about Dr. Gilmore, he will understand and I believe he will think it was time well spent when you tell him what you have been doing," the panda assured her.

Berry had always liked pandas and still owned the toy panda she had as a baby, so she figured it would be kind of fun to explore with this larger-than-life example of her soft and always-reliable toy friend.

"Come on, take my paw," the panda insisted. Berry tentatively took his paw and off they went together, climbing down into the woods below.

THE VILLAGE OF ILLUSIONS

They came to a clearing where there were several people sitting around eating. It looked as if the tables were made of chocolate and the chairs were made using pieces of candy canes. The trees were full of candies and licorice. What a magical place, she thought. On each of the chocolate tables, there was an enormous spread of food: apple pies, pecan pies, chocolate pies, fudge brownies and one of Berry's favorites, a whole plate of snowballs. Snowballs were chocolate covered with coconut on the outside and marshmallow on the inside. If you have never had one you have not lived, thought Berry. She could have eaten the entire plate herself.

As they walked closer, Berry began to notice that the people at the tables had a sickly look about them. She was surprised. She had felt sure with all these wonderful desserts that everyone would be happy. Instead, they all looked so glum, as if they had stomachaches. Berry asked panda about this and he said, "Well, you would think they would be happy, but the problem, Berry, is that this is the Land of Gluttony and Addiction. You can get too much of a good thing, you know."

"Oh, my goodness, that is really sad," declared Berry. "Can't they just get up and leave the table?"

"Well, yes they could," said panda thoughtfully, "but that would require them to make a commitment to live in the Land of Moderation and most of them are too full, too addicted, too lazy or too oblivious to make that effort. Then again, there could be other reasons that they keep eating. Sometimes people eat too much in order to comfort themselves and to avoid the pain they are really feeling. Things are not always as cut and dried as they look, you know," he said with a wry smile.

"What do you mean?"

"Well, for example, if a person feels rejected by others, perhaps they were rejected as a child and now as an adult they keep drawing rejection to them. Then they might overeat in order to cover up the pain," explained Panda.

Berry decided against reaching for the snowballs after all.

Panda suddenly took her hand and said, "Let's go, we have to meet your friends soon." They set off running through the woods.

Unknown to Berry, Veronica and Carmaletta were also in the woods that day and were having their own panda tours. Veronica was having a very similar experience to Berry, watching people eating lots and lots of wonderful desserts, except that Veronica saw them eating, while Berry saw them feeling sick after they had eaten.

"They must be very hungry to be eating so much," Veronica said.

"No," replied her companion, "they are eating to comfort themselves."

"Comfort themselves!" exclaimed Veronica. "Can't their parents do that for them?"

"Not always, and sometimes when we don't find affection where we need it, we look elsewhere," replied the panda.

Carmaletta had arrived in a room where everyone seemed as if they had shrunk compared to the furniture and fixtures around them. The refrigerator in the corner looked gigantic. There was an enormous table in the middle of the room filled with food and a giant cook top in the other corner. There were people walking around underneath the furniture. They did not seem very joyful, but they did not look entirely unhappy either. In fact, they seemed oblivious, in some sort of daze. If Carmaletta had not known better about the existence of the food above them, she would have suspected that they were unaware of their surroundings. Carmaletta was not tempted to eat the food herself. It looked very fattening.

"What is happening here?" she asked, with a perplexed look on her face.

"What do you see?" asked her furry black and white companion.

"I see very small people walking around, as if the food and surroundings above them are of no importance," she said.

"Ah, things are not always as they seem," said her new friend. "In fact, the people are somewhat aware of their surroundings, but they decided long ago that they did not deserve to eat regular meals, like other people. First they lost their sense of taste and then they lost their sense of smell, so I guess you could say they have kind of numbed out on food."

Carmaletta was alarmed at what she saw and something tweaked deep inside her stomach. She would pay attention to that another day, but for now, she was keen to have her questions answered.

"Are they stuck there forever? Can they get out? They look so grey and unwell and definitely not happy. Will they ever eat like regular people again?"

"Well, they could, but that would require their looking for help and talking about what is troubling them. Not always an easy thing to do," muttered the panda. "It is not so much what they eat as what is eating at them," he added thoughtfully.

Carmaletta looked at the panda quizzically and said, "Oh, that sounds oddly familiar. Perhaps I need to think about what is eating at me. I don't have a very good relationship with food either."

The panda smiled and told her they were going to meet up with her other two friends.

The Land of Moderation:

The three friends, along with their panda companions, met up at a coffee bar, which looked suspiciously like their favorite haunt.

"Where are we?" asked Carmaletta.

"This is the Town of Discipline, in the Land of Moderation," replied one of the pandas.

A waiter appeared and asked, "What would you like to order?" The girls looked at each other.

Veronica said, "Perhaps we could share a grilled chicken sandwich, Berry."

Carmaletta declared that she was going to have a chicken sandwich all to herself, but she was happy for her friends to share theirs. She took a deep breath and said, "I have some things that have been worrying me for some time. I know that I have been really mean to both of you about how much you eat, but the truth is that I have my own problems with food. I am afraid of getting fat and I am afraid of food, so I try not to eat. I worry all the time about my image and how I look and I believe I am making myself sick. I know I need help and I guess this is a good start by actually admitting it to my best friends."

"Oh, we will both support you in anyway that we can. Won't we, Berry?" said Veronica.

"Yes, of course, and maybe you can support us in living in the Land of Moderation from now on," added Berry.

The friends hugged and pledged to help each other.

Soon they found themselves back on the bridge where one of the senior boys was waiting for the latecomers. "You are late for school," he said. "You have to report to Dr. Gilmore's office right away." The three girls groaned and headed for the school building.

"Oh, no, now we are in trouble. I thought the panda said he would take care of that."

When they arrived in Dr. Gilmore's office, he was standing behind his desk, looking just as imposing and menacing as ever. "Well, girls, where have you been?" he asked in a deep voice.

"I am sorry we are late, sir," said Berry, "but we have been attending a seminar on the benefits of good nutrition and how to achieve a balanced life. We were learning about gluttony and addiction and also discipline and moderation."

"Yes, and we have been learning about the need to maintain a healthy body both mentally and physically," Carmaletta chimed in, quickly seeing where Berry was going.

Helen Turnbull, Ph. D.

Dr. Gilmore thought about this for a moment and said, "That sounds very impressive, girls. I am happy to see that you are so dedicated to your studies. Perhaps you would like to share your wisdom with your classmates and teachers today." Then he added, "But in future, don't be late."

"Oh yes, of course," cried the girls in unison. As they walked down the hallway with their arms around each other's shoulders, Dr. Gilmore watched them walk away. He smiled to himself. It was not always easy being the school Principal. He knew his reputation for being an ogre, but underneath his tough exterior, he really was a softy. He was just like the toffee pond he so carefully nurtured, a little tough when you first chew on them, but quite soft and pleasant once you have made the effort. It was just that he could not always afford to let people see that side of him. Perhaps he needed a visit to the forest and a conversation with the pandas himself.

Berry and her friends found themselves standing back at the edge of the toffee pond. Berry was not tempted to jump in the pond. She said goodbye to her friends, took off her shoes and socks, and carefully waded through, finding herself pretty quickly on the other side of the mirror with no evidence of toffee sticking to her. She reminded herself that being stuck in the toffee pond was not a good thing and that she would try not to do that in the future.

Berry felt as if she had been gone for ten days. She had most probably missed her flight. In fact, she was not, at that stage, convinced that she would ever find her way out of this adventure. She reflected on events and was certain of one thing; it had been quite a journey and certainly rated itself right up there with all of her other nomadic wanderings. It was a more exciting day's events than the meeting she was originally meant to attend.

She stepped outside into the sunlight, looked at her watch and discovered that she had only been inside for ten minutes. She would go and have a light lunch and sit and reflect on her day. She certainly had a lot to think about. When the day began, she thought she would have to spend it in Anywhere with nowhere to go, but now it felt as if she had spent the day somewhere with everywhere to go. As she looked down, she saw something glimmering at her feet. She bent down to pick it up and it was a batch of golden threads, similar to the ones that Ma Reflection had been using for her knitting. She carefully folded them and put them in her purse. Perhaps she would keep them as a reminder that she needed to stay focused on the positive patterns she had already developed and to be careful about the new patterns she would weave. As she sat having lunch, a morning dove flew past and a clock tower chimed way off in the distance.

Amethyst had been watching Patience's facial expressions for the past few minutes.

"So, Patience, what are you thinking?" she asked.

Patience grimaced. I am thinking it is time for me to wake up and for this dream to be over. That is what I am thinking, Amethyst," she said, somewhat defensively.

"If that is what you really want we can arrange for that to happen, Patience. After all, this is your dream." As she spoke, she raised her hand to snap her fingers. Patience realized what was about to happen.

"No, wait, Amethyst! I did not really mean that, it was just a kind of figure of speech. Sometimes I open my mouth and say things I don't really mean. Sorry! I am learning a lot about myself. I am not ready to wake up. What did you ask me? How did I feel about that story?"

Amethyst smiled and nodded in agreement.

"I am not sure where to start on this one. This story has a clear message for me and seems central to my struggles. Just like Berry, and all of the other women in the story, I have had my own struggles with self-image. I worry too much about too many things. On the surface I look like I am being cool, but lots of the time, I am worrying about what other people are thinking about me, and when I am feeling insecure and unhappy I use food to comfort me. I do not like it when people seem angry with me, especially men. I feel very threatened on those occasions. I know that does not make any sense, at least it doesn't to me, but that is what I do. Despite the fact that my left brain knows better, my right brain seems to be in charge at these moments. I cannot seem to stop myself from doing things that I know are sabotaging. It is crazy really, because sometimes I feel like I am doing it to spite other people who have hurt me and yet the only person I am hurting is myself. Go figure!" said Patience, finally running out of steam.

She sat quietly for a few minutes and then started to speak again.

"I guess I am rambling on in a stream of consciousness. This dream is really making me look at my behaviors and I must admit my brain is working overtime. I am not thrilled at what I am seeing. I wish I could believe that other people are the problem and that I am somehow exempt from all of their negative traits and behaviors, but the truth is that I am not. Every time I start to think it is about someone else, I then realize it also reminds me of me. Pretty sobering I would say!"

There was silence for a few minutes as Patience continued to reflect on the stories and then she spoke again.

"I keep trying to get a handle on my addiction to using food to comfort myself, but it is not easy. When I am feeling good about myself, I feel in control but it seems it does not take much to knock me off my base. Maybe I am dealing with rejection issues also, but I am not sure why. I cannot trace it back to any particular incident, but I do know that I get wound up when I feel people don't accept me. When I have a bad day and I run to the refrigerator for comfort, it is like a triple whammy. I feel instantly guilty, I do not feel good about myself, I do not really enjoy the food, I go to bed each night feeling like a failure and I am contributing to my weight gain, not to mention the incumbent health problems. So why do I do it?"

Her last question hung in the air unanswered as her voice trailed off.

Amethyst turned to her and said, "I think you are making more progress than you realize, Patience. It may not seem that way right now, but every journey begins with the first steps and you have made a start by acknowledging and owning your shortfalls and challenges."

Patience walked over to the nearest oak tree and tugged at some of the golden threads that were hanging around the trunk. "I had no idea how many of these threads were attached to me and how many anchors I have been dragging around. Perhaps I could take some of the threads home with me as a reminder that I need to stay focused on creating new and better patterns of behavior?"

"I am sure that can be arranged, Patience. Are you interested in reading another chapter?" asked Amethyst kindly.

Having vented a little, Patience was now able to move on and focus her energies on the next story.

"Lead the way, MacAmethyst!" she said, regaining her sense of humor and mustering her usual tenacity and vigor.

Chapter Three
The Village of Illusions

I never see you, I only see my version of you. (Seashore 2003)
The me that you see is not the me I believe myself to be.
(Turnbull 2003)

"Where are we now?" asked Patience.

"We are in the village square in the Village of Illusions," answered Amethyst.

"That is an interesting name for a village. How did they dream up a name like that?"

"Oh, I am sure we can find out quite a lot about this village before the evening is over, Patience."

"Someone is coming, let's ask them," exclaimed Patience as she ran towards Sam Spectator.

"Hi, my name is Patience, and this is Amethyst. What is yours?"

"Well, hi, Patience, I am Sam Spectator. What can I do for you today?" asked Sam in a grandfatherly tone.

"Tell us a little bit about your village please," asked Patience.

"Be glad to, young lady. Nothing I like better than to have a good natter about the village. I have lived here all my life and it is the best place to be."

"Illusions is a very unique and democratic village. The key to the village is the fact that all of its citizens own their own version of Illusions. We kind of know that everything is an illusion, if you know what I mean," said Sam with a laugh.

He reflected for a moment and then went on. "They do not always own up to knowing that everything is an illusion, but that is part of the

Helen Turnbull, Ph. D.

exotic charm about living here. No two people see Illusions in the same way. Sometimes they become convinced that their illusion is better than someone else's illusion. The Mayor and the people at the Village Hall used to oversee the growth of the village, but they have long since stopped trying due to lack of interest on our part. No one can agree on the direction things should go and everyone seems quite happy living with the status quo and blaming each other for it," explained Sam.

He continued. "In fact, that could also be said about the State of Reality, of which Illusions is a part, and indeed, of the entire country of Façade. It is exciting to live in such a diverse country, where everyone has their own views and is free to share them. The country looks like a very large piece of a jigsaw puzzle. There is a lot of national pride in being part of a country where everyone is, relatively speaking, free to determine the outcome of his or her own destiny. If there is a down side, no one appears to notice."

"What a fascinating place," exclaimed Patience. "What are these signs, Sam? They don't say anything."

"Oh, yes; one of the particularly charming facets of the village is that all of the signposts point in many directions with no particular destinations on them. It is entirely up to the individual which path they decide to walk each day. Most people find it exciting, not knowing where they will end up, but a few people find it distressing. They would prefer guidance that is more direct. The others tease them and tell them they should be living in the State of Compulsion or Control and not the State of Reality," laughed Sam.

THE VILLAGE OF ILLUSIONS

"The Village Square, where we are standing, is a good place to meet others. We are a friendly community and people enjoy getting together."

Sam really loved the village and could talk about it almost ad nauseam. Patience was beginning to think that she was getting more information than she needed, but she did not want to seem impolite.

"The village you describe feels like it is the center of the universe," said Patience.

"Well, young lady, perhaps not, but it is the center of my universe. We can be a little myopic; after all, we are a village!" Sam said with a laugh.

Sam became lost in his own thoughts. He reflected on what Patience had just said. He knew that people in the village sensed that they were part of something much larger, intuitively knowing when they looked outside, that they had a part to play in a bigger picture. Ironically, however, most of them did not own a passport and had very little desire to travel further than Reality and a few nearby States. They knew that in the other countries they had allies and adversaries. They used to speak of being courageous enough to venture forth, wondering aloud what it would be like to learn more about their allies. Did they look like them and think like them? Did they speak the same language, eat the same food, and listen to the same music? They also worried and wondered why anyone would be their adversary and determined that one day they should try to learn more. For now, however, they were content to remain where they were. It felt safer and more secure.

One of the unique things about living in the Village of Illusions was that people could live in different States simultaneously. Mrs. Baker, for example, lived in the State of Reality, the State of People-Pleasing and the State of Neediness almost all of the time, with more than the occasional visit to the State of Anxiety (Aronson 1999). Many of the citizens had winter homes in some of these other States and spent long periods there. By way of balance, people also ensured that they spent some time in their summer homes visiting States such as Tranquility, Happiness and Joy. It was an interesting phenomenon, however, that they seemed to spend less time in their summer homes than they did in their winter homes.

Their national bird was the morning dove. People were very enthralled by this bird and knew that when it flew it carried important messages. They had heard that somewhere in the "old country" long ago, they used pigeons to convey messages to people. That was before the days of the internet and cyberspace, of course, and they thought it was a quaint habit. Out of respect for their history and connectedness to the old country, they had decided to honor the morning dove by making it their national bird.

The mayor had told them that the dove is a bird of prophecy and can help you to see what you can give birth to in your life.[1]

Today was a very special day in the Village of Illusions, particularly because it was always "today." The villagers remembered yesterdays and could always look forward to tomorrows, but they really only lived for today, which they proudly thought was the way it should be. On this particular today, the Village Square was buzzing with people scurrying back and forth. There was a big sports event that evening at the local arena. The local soccer team, The Illusionists, was playing against a neighboring team, The Figments, and the village was buzzing with excitement.

In the middle of the Square, right outside the Village Hall, there was a wonderful gnarly, old bench made from an oak tree. Despite its appearance, it was surprisingly comfortable to sit on. Sam and his wife, Sally Spectator, were quite often to be found in their usual seats on the bench watching the world go by. Sam and Sally had turned sitting there into an art form. They were such an established feature that when people saw the bench they expected to see Sam and Sally. Sam and Sally went shopping every morning and then made their way to the bench, where they would spend an enjoyable few hours just watching their neighbors as they passed by and talking to people about their lives and the day's events. Today was no exception as Sam said goodbye to Patience and Amethyst and set off towards the bench to meet his wife.

Sally Spectator was an elegant looking woman who had aged well. She had mousy brown hair and pale blue eyes. She had a lovely smile and a charismatic energy, which always made people feel that she was interested in them. Sally was very much an extrovert and loved to talk. People always knew what Sally was thinking. Sam on the other hand, was more of an introvert and had the kind of face that was difficult to read. It was almost as if his facial muscles did not move, and yet when he smiled or laughed he could make the room light up and everyone would feel the warmth of his mood. He had a compassionate nature, but was more inclined to keep his thoughts to himself than Sally was. He was a handsome man and was ageing gracefully. He looked quite distinguished with his tall stature and silver-grey hair.

Illusions was a tight-knit community where people knew each other. "Downright neighborly", that is what people called it. Sometimes it might feel a little too imposing and perhaps "nosy" was another word for neighborly, but for the most part people felt secure in the knowledge that everyone knew them and knew enough about their business to care about them. If anyone was sick, for example, they could count on Mrs. Baker dropping by with some of her infamous chicken soup, some vitamins and a handful of friendly advice. If anyone needed to leave town they could always count on their neighbors to watch over their house and to take care of their pets. Ms. Cosmopolitan particularly appreciated the caring nature of this small community. She traveled a lot on business and visited many interesting places. It was always fun to listen to her stories when she returned. She did not have any pets or children to look after, but she did welcome knowing that her neighbors would take care of her mail and keep a watchful eye on her house. Not everyone was wonderful, of course; some people were harder to love than others. Carmaletta Spatts, for example, was difficult to predict. Some days she would be friendly and engaging and say nice things, and other days she would say things that were thoughtless and unkind or she would just walk right on by as if you did not exist. Everyone in the village knew that and as tiresome as it was, they would just wait to see which Carmaletta would show up each day.

Sam and Sally had arrived at the bench around 11:30 a.m. Sally had just been to the village store for their daily shopping and had brought Sam a copy of *Today*, the village newspaper. Sam would peer over the top of the paper to see all of the passersby. He could count on Sally to keep him well informed whenever someone really interesting was coming or indeed if she spotted something happening that was worthy of a little extra attention.

"You know, Sally, I met two very interesting ladies a little while back. They said their names were Patience and Amethyst. I had never seen them here before. I guess they are newcomers. We are not too keen on newcomers as you know, but they seemed like nice people and one of them was particularly interested in the village."

"Oh, that is nice, Sam, I am glad you talked with them. It is good to make people feel welcome," said Sally, scanning the square as she spoke.

Just at that moment, she spotted Joe Fixit rushing across the square.

"Hi, Joe, where are you off to in such a rush?" she called.

Joe's brow furrowed. Oh, bother, just what I need when I am in a hurry. Now I need to stop and have a conversation with the Spectators and they will want to know all of my business. My wife will be upset if she hears that I rushed past without speaking to them. After all, they are one of the village treasures, almost like an informal Mayor and Mayoress. He laughed at himself as he thought about that image. Joe was all of six feet two inches tall and towered over Sam and Sally as they sat. He was about to celebrate his 55th birthday and thought of himself as a seasoned businessman. He had a friendly disposition and was always ready with a cheerful smile for people, but behind the thin layer of congeniality lurked a much more intense personality and when he was busy, which he often was, he had a tendency to become quite controlling and demanding. His listening skills were not the best and he had a habit of asking questions and never hearing the answers.

"I am doing just fine, Sally. Thank you for asking. I am rushing off to find some extra tickets for tonight's match. I have some business colleagues in town. I am definitely going to the game and it would be awkward to leave my guests in the hotel. Not good for business, you know!"

"Oh, I see, Joe," said Sally. "Well, at least I think I do." She truthfully did not have the slightest interest in soccer and could not really understand why people were making such a big deal of this match.

Sam's head popped up from the top of his newspaper. "Hi, Joe, it's going to be a great match tonight. I'm going to watch it on television, but I kind of wish I was going now that the excitement is mounting. How are Mrs. Fixit and the kids?"

"Doing fine last time I checked," said Joe. "To be honest with you I am so busy at work these days that I hardly have time for my family. A man has to do what a man has to do. You know that, Sam," he said in his most masculine voice. The two men exchanged knowing nods.

Just at that moment, Mrs. Baker came walking past. "Hi, everyone," she called cheerfully. "What a beautiful morning. How are you today, Sally? Did you get that email I sent you? I'm off to a very important meeting at the Village Hall." She moved closer to Sally, almost as if she were whispering. "There are a few things going on there that I don't like and I have decided to speak out. There is no point in keeping quiet. Nothing ever changes if you keep quiet. I spend my life trying to be appropriate you know, not hurting anyone's feelings and what thanks do you get for it? Might as well tell people what you really think. Don't you agree, Sally?"

Mrs. Baker was a very jolly woman with a friendly disposition and an enormous amount of generosity. She always had a cheerful word for people, and seemed genuinely interested in their well-being. She had beautiful red hair and a round face with polished cheeks and smiling green eyes. She had exceptionally good taste in clothes and was always impeccably dressed. Sally guessed that Mrs. Baker was probably in her mid 60's. She was a very attractive woman, Rubenesque in her appearance, and in recent years had been worrying constantly about her weight.

"I hope your meeting goes well, Mrs. Baker. It sounds as if you have a very important mission to accomplish." Sally was reeling a little from Mrs. Baker's rapid-fire questions, but she knew that Mrs. Baker had a good heart and always meant well, so she agreed with her and wished her good luck.

Helen Turnbull, Ph. D.

Sam's head had disappeared behind his paper, but Mrs. Baker spotted him and said, "Hello, Sam. How are you today? Are you checking the news? Are you reading anything interesting? Did you hear that Mr. Funds, the Bank Manager has decided to retire? What a shame, he was always so helpful with his customers. We will miss him, don't you think? Do you think the Illusionists can win tonight? I am not so sure. I think that the Figments are the better team. I hate to admit it. Mr. Baker is going to the match, so I hope they win for his sake. He gets grouchy when his team loses. Huh! Come to think of it, he gets grouchy over a lot of things. Maybe it is for my sake that I hope they win. The thought of him coming home grouchy does not exactly fill me with glee. He once threatened to kick our television out of the window when his team lost, so I usually route for them to win. Can't blame me, can you? Must run or I will be late. See you later."

Sam slid back behind his paper, relieved that he had not had to answer any of Mrs. Baker's rhetorical questions.

In the midst of all this conversation, Joe Fixit had rushed off, unnoticed, in the hopes of purchasing his extra tickets for the big match. Sam and Sally settled down on their bench to enjoy the sunshine and a browse of the morning newspaper. The birds were playing around their feet and there were a couple of morning doves and blue jays flying back and forth across the square, as if they were looking for something. Sally commented to Sam that she had never seen the morning doves and blue jays flying in concert before. It was as if they were hanging out together, working on a project or something.

Sam told her not to be so ridiculous. "You have too fanciful an imagination, woman," he scolded her kindly. "Come on, let's go and have some lunch."

OVERLOOKING THE VILLAGE SQUARE

They picked up their groceries and Sam's newspaper and wandered off in the direction of their favorite local restaurant. When the weather was nice, as it was today, they liked to sit at a table outside, where they could continue to watch the comings and goings. On the way there, they bumped into Berry Cosmopolitan.

"Hello, Berry. You look very nice today. Are you off on your travels again?" asked Sally.

"Oh, hello, Mrs. Spectator. Yes, I am off on another business trip. I have a plane to catch in about four hours and as usual I am rushing around at the last minute," gasped Berry.

Berry Cosmopolitan was a very attractive woman. She had short dark hair and piercing blue eyes. She was 45 years old, this week in fact. She was not a small woman in either stature or physical size. When Berry walked into a room people knew she was there. She was charismatic and her energy seemed to fill up the space around her. She was highly regarded in her professional life, but in the privacy of her own mind, her self-image did not always match what she projected. She constantly struggled with self-confidence. Her mother, who was much more petite than she was, always reminded her that she "took after her Father's side of the family." Berry told herself she was just big-boned, but truthfully, she did not believe that and always struggled with the way she looked. Other people saw her as extremely intelligent, always well dressed, professional, friendly, generous to a fault and willing to lend a helping hand to others.

"Do you have time to join us for lunch? You would be most welcome," said Sam with a friendly smile. He liked Berry. She was a hard worker; she made stimulating conversation and was a person with a kind heart. He enjoyed teasing her and discussing politics with her and she could always hold her own in the conversation. Sally used to get upset at him for discussing politics with Berry, so he usually had to be a little more circumspect than he wanted, just to keep the peace.

"I would love to do that, Sam, but I am meeting Carmaletta and Veronica for a quick lunch. Maybe another day, but thanks," she said as she rushed off.

"Everyone is in such a rush today, Sam. I'm glad you and I can move at a more leisurely pace," said Sally, clutching Sam's arm. "I worry that all the rushing that people are doing might mean they are losing something."

"What on earth do you mean, Sally? Is this another one of your flights of fancy?"

"Not exactly," said Sally. "Well, at least I don't think it is. I have just been observing that people seem to have less time for each other than they used to have. I remember when people used to sit down with us on the bench and we would have a good long chat about their families and how things were going and now no one has any time to stop. If they do stop, it is only for a few minutes and they spend half the time explaining to us where they are rushing off to and why they cannot stop for long. I even heard the other day that some of our friends were complaining about taking too long to play golf. They said it took four hours and fifteen minutes. That doesn't seem too long to me. Why are they rushing anyway?"

"People are busy, you know, they are not all retired like us."

"I know, I know, but I am worried that we are missing something very precious by rushing through our lives."

"Like what?"

Sam had learned long ago that when his wife was in this mood the best thing to do was to ask questions, listen and look interested. Telling her she was talking rubbish was never a good move.

"Well, like our ability to care for each other; our ability to be interested in each other; the art of conversation, our sense of contentment, our sense of community, maybe even our overall sense of happiness," said Sally with a very serious look on her face.

"Yikes, Sally! You are worrying about some very big issues. You may be right, though. I have also been feeling an increasing emptiness about our conversations at the bench. It is not the same. People do not have as much time for each other. I guess they call this progress, but now that you mention it, I am not so sure. What do you think we should do about it?"

"I don't think we can do anything about it, Sam. I think it will take people much more important than us to fix this. It is a much bigger problem than we can solve."

"You know, Sam, I cannot imagine my life without you. We spend time together and we talk about all the things that matter to us. You are my best friend. And yet, I have this nagging feeling that people have lost the ability to appreciate the little things in life. To be able to value each other's company, to really enjoy having a conversation.

They both fell silent, living with their own thoughts and concerns about the picture Sally had just painted.

Suddenly their tranquil silence was interrupted.

"It's not fair! Why do I always have to do this?" exclaimed the young girl as she stomped past Sam and Sally's table.

"What is all the commotion about, Victoria? You look like someone has just stolen your universe," said Sam kindly.

"My little brother is missing again and I always get sent to find him. It's not fair."

THE VILLAGE OF ILLUSIONS

"Where do you think he has gone this time?" asked Sally, who was familiar with the repetitive nature of this situation.

"Oh, I don't know. He usually goes down to the woods to play with his friends and I hate going down there to find him. It gives me the creeps. Why does he always get away with so many things? They would not let me run off like that. Boys get more freedom than girls." Victoria continued to complain. "They make me wash the dishes every night after dinner and he just goes out to play."

Sally laughed and tried to console the young girl. Knowing that the "they" to whom Victoria referred were her well-meaning parents, she said, "Well, it may be too late for my generation, but I am sure things are going to change for yours. Women will have more freedom and more rights than I ever had. And you know, your parents are teaching you to be responsible and learning responsibility is never a bad thing."

"Huh, I suppose so, Mrs. Spectator, but you sound just like my mother. I hate being the eldest, because all I am ever expected to be is RESPONSIBLE!" she said, as she ran off down the street in search of her intrepid brother.

Sam and Sally watched as Victoria disappeared into the distance. They set off to walk home and came across Mrs. Rover. Oh dear, thought Sally. Mrs. Rover is lost again. She got lost a lot these days and it was very worrying for her and her family. It was fortunate that the community all knew her and knew where she lived, so whenever anyone found her they could always direct her back home.

"Hello, Mrs. Rover, how are you today?" asked Sally. "Are you looking for something?"

"Yes!" said Mrs. Rover in a frustrated tone. "I have run out of groceries and refreshments and I could have sworn that the grocery store was here, but now I can't seem to find it."

"That is annoying," said Sally in a conciliatory tone. "Actually, the grocery store is just round the corner. Shall we walk there with you and then walk you home?" she asked.

"That would be very nice of you, dear. I would like that," said Mrs. Rover with a tentative smile.

Despite her years, Ella Rover had aged very well. She was slim and petite and prided herself in her immaculate appearance. She would never be seen out of doors without make up and she always wore dainty sandals on her feet, which were not good for walking, but they made her feel good. Physically she was in very good shape for her age. Her big problem these days was that her short term memory was beginning to lapse. She was a fiercely independent woman and she intensely disliked the idea that she now had to be dependent on other people. However, the trouble was that when she left the house intent on going somewhere, she quite often forgot where she was going, or even worse, she forgot how to get home again. She knew people were being kind and were trying to help her, but sometimes she just wanted to scream and run away. Maybe return to the "old country," where she felt she really belonged. She wanted to tell them that she could do it herself, but in her heart, she knew that was no longer true. Nowadays she spent a lot of time thinking about the past and reliving her happier memories. She had really loved her father and she enjoyed talking about him. She had loved her husband and since he died, she missed him terribly, even all these years later. He had been a good husband and father and no one else had ever matched up to him, so she had chosen to live alone for many years. It is OK living alone, most of the time, and each evening she would comfort herself with a little refreshment, just the way she used to do when her husband was alive.

"They keep taking my house keys!" she exclaimed to Sally. "I am really very angry, just because I am old does not mean I am stupid."

"Oh dear, Ella, I am sure you have just misplaced your keys and they will turn up soon," said Sally.

Sally knew that Ella kept hiding her purse and her keys and that her daughters had had so many extra keys made. The problem was that not only did Ella not remember where she hid the keys, she did not remember hiding them at all.

Sam and Sally helped Mrs. Rover buy her groceries and then they patiently walked her home. All the way home Ella talked about the past, remembering events in her life and recounting the milestones along the way.

"I remember the day they crowned me Queen," she said with a smile that covered her entire face. "They told me my real mother came to see me that day, but she never spoke to me."

Sally had heard the story before, but she knew how important that event was for Ella so she listened compassionately as if she were hearing it for the first time.

On the way to their home Sally said, "You know, Sam, it has been a funny day. Everything that happened today was about people rushing through their lives and people being lost. I wonder what that means."

Sam put a friendly arm around his wife's shoulders. "My dearest, Sally, you have a heart bigger and warmer than the sun and a mind that is more curious than an encyclopedia. That is why I love you so much. But for tonight, let's take a break from worrying about other people and just go home and enjoy our dinner." Sally smiled knowingly to herself as they walked towards the comfort of their home, casting one last quizzical look back towards the four birds now sitting on the tree at the bottom of her driveway.

[1] *Because of its association with Goddesses, it was considered the embodiment of the maternal instinct. The name "dove" has been given to oracles and to prophets, such as Jonah or the Dove. (Andrews 2001).*

Chapter Four
The Lost Brother

Why build a shack for yourself in your imagination, when you could build a Palace. (Photiou 2001)

The Circus:

"Victoria, go and find your brother. I told him not to wander off and he has done it again," her mother called to her from the kitchen window. Victoria was playing happily in the back garden. The circus was in town and Victoria knew that there was a high percentage chance that her younger brother had followed the lunchtime parade down to the local fairground. She had heard him talking to his friends about it earlier that day.

She sighed at the predictability of it all and took off to look for her brother. It was not the first time and probably would not be the last time she would have to put her own needs aside and look for him. She set off down Main Street towards an area called The Palace Grounds, aptly named in acknowledgement of the Crystal Palace on the Island State of Inner Wisdom. This was the area where all the big public events in the village happened. The circus came there once a year.

The elephants were leading the parade, so she followed them. She liked elephants. There was something grand and imposing about them, and yet at the same time they were lumbering and clumsy, a sort of analogy for life. She had read somewhere that *elephants show great affection and loyalty to each other and older calves will help younger siblings. (Andrews 2001).* How appropriate, she thought, as she continued scanning the crowd looking for her younger brother, Astar.

The clowns came behind the elephants, doing what clowns do best, fooling around and trying to make people laugh. She was not too sure about clowns. She always felt as if clowns looked strange and that perhaps they were laughing for the wrong reasons, or they were laughing when they really wanted to be crying. Who were they behind all that make up? She was convinced that behind the facade of a clown there were other faces with very real issues. They wore masks that she did not trust. Maybe we all wear masks.

As she approached the gates and saw the circus tents, animals and clowns, she was intrigued and could well understand the lure this must have provided for her brother and his friends. Circus people were mysterious people. Adults around her said they were traveling people. She did not really know what that meant, but the way they said, it always sounded ominous. She was a little afraid of them, scared they might steal her brother if she did not find him soon.

The circus people were busy setting up their tents and their sideshows. There were many trucks parked on the grass and very large cables running from the trucks to where the tents would be. She gingerly stepped over the cables and made her way towards the main tent. The cages with the animals were set up behind the tent. As she walked around the side she saw two llamas walking towards her, thankfully on a leash managed by an attendant. Behind them in the distance were the cages with the lions and tigers. I shall stay far away from them, she thought.

Where was her brother? What a nuisance it was wandering around in this unknown territory because someone you cared about was lost. I guess the question she had was whether he was really lost, or just on his own path. She could not relate to the path he had chosen. Nor apparently, could her mother, as she was always sending her to find him. He seemed oblivious to their concerns, however, as he continued to walk his own course.

It is a funny thing about brothers, if you are sister, that is. They do not think as you do. They do not seem to have the same interests as you. In fact, they act as if you are an inconvenience to them most of the time. They certainly live in a different world, she thought to herself.

Her brother, in the meantime, was having the most amazing time. He had spotted the circus entourage about an hour before Victoria, so he had quite a head start on her in terms of his adventure. He had persuaded two of his school chums, Boyd and Archie, to come with him and they had set off down Main Street towards the Palace Grounds. Astar was the leader of their group. He felt very important and had a great sense of adventure. He had a vivid imagination and would often tell great stories about his escapades with the other boys at school. His mother had warned him earlier that morning not to follow the circus that day, but at this moment, these particular instructions were not accessible to his conscious mind. He was quite oblivious to any consternation he might cause. Of more concern to him was the height of the giraffe and the speed with which it was lunging down Main Street.

When a giraffe comes into your life you should ask yourself "are you seeing the consequences of your words and deeds?" (Andrews 2001).

ELEPHANT AND GIRAFFE

Astar was not thinking about consequences as he ran on ahead of his friends, anxious to get there and explore as much as he could. His two friends were running on his heels trying to keep up. As they reached the circus tent they were out of breath, but still curious. They ran behind the tent and bumped into a man who was tending to the animals.

"What have we here?" he said, grabbing Astar by the collar. "Perhaps you would like to help us feed the animals?" he asked with a sinewy smile.

He walked the three boys into another tent where some men were huddled in a corner. The three boys did not know whether to be scared or excited. Perhaps a bit of both.

"Here," said the man, pushing the three boys towards the group, "some helping hands."

The men laughed and invited the three boys to come and join them for a soda.

The boys were looking forward to seeing the animals, so after they drank their sodas the men offered to show them around.

In the meantime, Victoria had begun to worry and made up a story about what was happening to her brother. She could not find him and she was becoming increasingly convinced that he had been abducted by those people at the circus.

She sat down on a park bench that was on the dividing line between the tennis courts and the circus grounds to think about what to do next.

In the haze of the afternoon sun, a woman who looked like a gypsy walked towards her. She said, "Are you looking for your brother, my dear?"

Victoria was immediately scared and shaken. What did this woman know that she did not? "Yes, I am looking for my brother," she said.

"Well, you are a little too late. Some of the circus folks have taken him and his two friends on to their next town. He will be made to work for them there and then...," her voice trailed off.

"That can't be," yelled Victoria. "He is my brother. You can't do that."

"No use yelling at me, young lady," said the woman in a scolding tone. "He shouldn't have been wandering where he wasn't wanted." She looked thoughtful for a moment and then, more pragmatically than informatively, she said, "He doesn't fit in very well, he's a little too posh for them, but the circus folks, you know, they need help and they'll take all the help they can get. If you ever want to see him again you had better come with me."

Victoria was terrified, but she reluctantly followed the woman, her knees knocking, but powerless to resist. The woman led her towards a motorcycle with a sidecar and beckoned her to get in. Victoria was not so sure about this, but found herself hesitantly climbing on board anyway. Off they sped down what looked like a country lane. After a very fast and exhilarating ride, they arrived at a village green where there were a number of candy-colored tents adorning the lawn. The woman pulled the bike and sidecar over to the edge of the village green, jumped off and started walking rapidly away, indicating as she did for Victoria to follow her. The woman disappeared into one of the tents and Victoria had to run to catch up with her.

Once inside the tent she saw the circus ring filled with sawdust. There were some clowns in the middle of the ring holding umbrellas and fooling

Helen Turnbull, Ph. D.

around on bicycles. One of them had his umbrella up, but it was broken and provided him no protection. The other had his umbrella upside down. A third clown came across and pushed the first one off his bicycle. The first clown was very friendly and funny and he was clowning around with the others, generally being the ringleader and helping the others to laugh and have fun. If they fell, he helped them up again; when they stumbled, he rushed over to stop them from falling. Then he would take out a water pistol and squirt them, falling down in gales of laughter. He seemed to be the most loveable and she laughed along with them.

The second clown seemed to get into the most trouble. He climbed off his bicycle and picked up a ladder that he kept trying to climb up, but since he did not lean it against anything, he kept falling down. Repeatedly he tried, but each time to no avail. It was funny and yet frustrating to watch. She wanted so badly to tell the clown to come over and lean the ladder against something stable and yet as she looked around the tent there was nothing there. Well, maybe a pole, but where would that take him?

THE VILLAGE OF ILLUSIONS

CLOWN SCENE

The third clown was sitting on an upside down paint bucket looking very mournful, sobbing and laughing simultaneously. The other two clowns tried to comfort him, but he seemed not to be able to engage with them, always moving just out of their reach.

As she continued to watch them, the third clown starting tumbling repeatedly and the faster he tumbled it seemed he was going to plough into the second clown. Just as she was going to cry out to warn them, the third clown disappeared, almost as if he had merged into the other. She was wide-eyed with amazement as she watched the second clown start to tumble and then bump into the first; fading into him until there was only one clown left standing. It was the most lovable clown who was still standing. He turned to her and took three bows. She did not know whether to laugh or cry she was so astonished. She bowed her head and acknowledged his, or rather, their performance.

As she was recovering from this experience, she heard a noise overhead and she looked up to see someone on the trapeze above her head. She moved to the side to watch as the performer swung proficiently from one bar to the other. She did not mind heights, nor did she mind taking risks, but she thought the risk of hanging from a trapeze without a safety net was nothing short of foolish. The trapeze artist swung from the bars onto a high wire and picked up a large pole. He then competently and carefully walked the full length of the high wire. When he turned to walk back, he missed his footing and slipped. She was horrified and closed her eyes, feeling he was going to come crashing to the ground. However, when she opened them again she saw him dangling in front of her, lowering himself to the ground from a safety cord attached to his back. Wow, what a narrow escape, she thought. How many times had he fallen and recovered?

She got up to walk away, deciding that she did not really enjoy circus life, too many things to worry about. Victoria woke up and found that she was still sitting on the park bench. She blinked and looked at her watch; it had only been five minutes. How could that be? She must have fallen asleep and been dreaming. She started walking towards the circus people again and this time she spotted her brother and his friends helping to feed the animals. She ran over to him and told him that he had to come home. He was pleased to see her and asked her to join them.

"No, we need to go home now, Astar," she protested.

He laughed and said, "I'm fine really, I'm having fun. I will come home with my friends when I am ready. Tell Mum I am OK."

The Elephant and the Giraffe:

Victoria reluctantly set off home without Astar. At least she could tell her mother that she knew where he was. She was feeling quite shaken from the experience. She did not like the circus or the people in it. She did not like the fact that her brother seemed to be in their world, not hers, and

THE VILLAGE OF ILLUSIONS

she did not like the fact that she had had to spend her afternoon searching for him when he did not want to be found. Eventually she realized that he was having fun his way. She rationalized, even when he was not having fun, it would have to be his nightmare, not hers. As she left the Palace Grounds, she saw the gypsy woman leaning against the gate. She waved to her and smiled. Had she been daydreaming? Alternatively, had it been real after all?

What was she dealing with? Was it her worst fears? His worst fears? Her worst fears on his behalf. Or was it just her reality, the stories she made up in her head? She was not quite sure. She was sure that making up a story about what someone else was going through was not very productive. She was going to try to live in the present from now on, only dealing with what was happening. The only person she had been able to control on this trip was herself and even that had been questionable at times. Pragmatically, she thought she was more like the elephant, caring for her siblings, grand and imposing, lumbering and clumsy. From her perspective, Astar was like the giraffe, not looking at the ramifications of his actions. Just like the giraffe, he had his feet and legs on the ground and his head in the air, but maybe that was not so bad. He certainly had a different view of things from up there. She shrugged her shoulders. What she was going to tell her mother was quite another issue, but as they all had their own version of reality, it probably did not matter anyway. Astar's version would be taller and more exciting than hers was by far. She knew that for sure. As she walked home she pondered who really was lost.

Patience could not wait to add her interpretation to this story. "You know, Amethyst, I have a brother also. In some ways, I feel the same way about him as Victoria does about her brother. He has chosen a course for himself that has not always been easy to watch and even less easy to be a part of. I gave up trying a long time ago and just resigned myself to the fact that I could not face my own pain about what I saw happening to him and I could not live his life for him, but I confess it hurts to watch and I miss him. He is angry and he always seems to be sabotaging himself. He is very intelligent and a kind person underneath the facade he puts out to the world and I kind of wish he could rediscover that person. Maybe then he would be more available to the rest of us," Patience said wistfully. "In the meantime, the lesson I really learn from this story is that while we all make up stories in our heads about the rights and wrongs of other people's lives, the truth is that we have no control and cannot live their lives for them. Just like all the other stories, it also makes me realize that there are probably people looking at my life and wishing I would do it differently and perhaps feeling frustrated at the decisions I have made in

Helen Turnbull, Ph. D.

my life. They may not be wrong, but it does not matter; only I can change that. Sometimes, just like the lost brother, I feel lost, even to myself. I am not exactly a failure, far from it, I have accomplished a lot, but there are definitely things I wish I had done differently. Actually, there have been people over the years that did not deserve a front row seat in my life and I let them have one for too many years. I think I am getting better about that though," said Patience reflectively.

Chapter Five
Queen of Illusions

Wasted talents are like sundials in the shade.
(Benjamin Franklin)

Be tender with the young, compassionate with the aged, and tolerant with the weak and wrong. Sometime in life you have been all of these.
(Bob Goddard)

"I was Queen of Illusions, you know," she said for the umpteenth time. "They crowned me Queen that day and they told me that my real mother came to see me. They said she was in the crowd. I wish she had come to say hello, but she never did and I do not know who she is. To this day, that is my one real regret, not knowing my real mother." Her fragile voice trailed off into the atmosphere.

Her children, with compassion and benign tolerance, rolled their eyes, listening once again to her story, which they had heard so often.

She had indeed been Queen of the Village of Illusions. That was in the mid-1930s, but they had long since stopped that ceremony. In fact, she even had the distinction of being the first Queen of Illusions. There is no record of how many came after her, so as far as she was concerned and certainly from her children's perspective, she was THE Queen of Illusions.

Ella Rover was a very attractive woman. Even at the age of 79, she was trim, petite and beautiful. She had a very pretty face and prided herself in dressing well. Even on her worst days, she could be seen walking to the grocery store in gold-studded sandals, which might be inappropriate for walking long distances, but they looked good and that was important to her.

One day her granddaughter jokingly said to her, "Grandma, I am a Princess, you know."

Everyone laughed and her mother responded, "We are all Princesses in this family." Ella's 79-year-old ears perked up as she sat straight up in the chair and said, "Actually, no, that is not true – I am not a Princess, I am a Queen. They crowned me Queen of Illusions you know. My real mother was there that day......"

Everyone smiled in agreement and the conversation shifted to other issues. As Ella listened to her daughters talking about their various professional careers she said, "You are all so clever, and you have all had such incredible opportunities. In my day, there were no big opportunities for women to have their own education or career. I guess that is why I am not as clever as you are."

One of her daughters asked her, "Why did you not try to find your real mother?"

"Oh, I would never do that," she exclaimed. "I did not want to upset anyone."

I wonder how your life would have been different if you had done that? I wonder how your life would have changed if Dad had not died so young? Would your life have been different if you had had a formal education? I wonder what incredible opportunities would have opened up for you? I wonder how your being different would have changed us?

These thoughts never passed anyone's lips. Perhaps there was no point in asking; it was too late to change things now anyway. Even if she lived another twenty years, how would asking her these questions change anything?

Bracketing Reality:

Ella found herself at the age of 12 cleaning house for a very demanding, intolerant and lazy mother, a woman who had adopted both her and her brother. Ella's only comforts in life were her relationship with her adoptive father, whom she adored, and her cat, Billy. Some of her friends nicknamed her Cinders and used to tease her about how much house cleaning she had to do.

She was crowned the Queen of Illusions when she was 12. She was very proud to have been selected. There had been stiff competition that year. She was a very pretty girl, even if she was inordinately shy and insecure. The day that she wore her crown and rode on the cart to the ceremony was one of the proudest days of her life. Everyone noticed her and she probably felt more important that day than she ever had before. She liked getting this kind of attention and it certainly made a change from all the negative attention she was used to getting at home. Realizing what it felt like to be Queen for the day, being the center of attention and adulation, set patterns in motion that played out for the rest of her life. It felt good not to be the Cinderella she characterized at home. She had no ugly stepsisters, but she certainly had an unreasonably demanding mother (or wicked witch, depending on her mood that day). For now, however, there was no Prince Charming in sight. Well, not in direct sight at least.

Helen Turnbull, Ph. D.

CORONATION

Down at the Pond:

Senior Turtle and Octogenarian, the elderly turtles in Amethyst's garden, had just spoken with Woody and heard all about Ella Rover. One of their favorite things to do was to take a story that Woody had told them about his recent adventures and then reframe it to have another outcome. Today it was Octogenarian's turn to read. Everyone settled down at the edge of the pond, the animals were seated on the grass and the fish were swaying gently in the warm water close to the surface. Octogenarian began to read....

She wanted to go and see her, to see what kind of young woman she had grown to be. She had heard that she was very beautiful and was a hard worker. She was very proud of her and was deeply saddened that she had not been allowed to keep her. In these days, it was very shameful to have a baby out of wedlock. (It should still be shameful now, thought Octogenarian, but times had changed since he was a young turtle).

She walked through the crowd to get a closer look. What a beautiful young woman she saw, standing upright with a shy smile on her face; looking, nevertheless, as if she had been born into royalty. She watched as the Queen of Illusions was crowned. The Queen waved to the crowd and her birth mother applauded as loudly as anyone did.

She waited at the end of the ceremony and as the newly crowned Queen walked towards her she moved forward and said, "Hello, congratulations on being crowned Queen today. You looked very beautiful. I am a cousin of your mother's, my name is Margaret and I was wondering if we could stop and have a coffee together."

It seemed like a strange request to the new Queen; here was a perfect stranger inviting her to coffee and yet she intuitively knew that it was OK to accept. They both walked together in a comfortable silence to the coffee shop that was next door to the local butcher's.

As they talked and became acquainted with each other, time seemed to stand still. Ella felt so comfortable with this woman and could not understand why. She had never before been in the company of a woman who made her feel safe. Usually she did not trust anyone, particularly a woman. They laughed together, drank more coffee and talked for a long time.

As they were getting ready to part company the older woman seemed to take a very deep breath and then cleared her throat a couple of times. Ella could tell she was trying to say something and she looked at her in anticipation.

"Ella, I have something to say. I don't know if I am doing the right thing, but I feel compelled to tell you," she said. Her face flushed bright red and she dropped her eyes to the ground.

What? Ella was feeling anxious for the first time since meeting her.

The woman took another deep breath and said, "I am your birth mother, and I want you to know that I love you very much and I would have loved to have been allowed to keep you, but they would not let me. I hope you will always be very happy and that you will always know that I love you."

Ella was taken aback. She could not quite believe what she was hearing and yet she knew that it was true.

"I don't know what to say. I am very pleased to meet you, I am sure," stammered Ella.

"If you are my real mother, then who is the woman I call my mother?"

"The woman you know as your mother is my aunt. She is a very good and kind woman. She has a lot of kindness in her heart and she sacrificed a lot to raise both you and your half brother. I know she is not always easy to get along with, but she means well and she has done an excellent job of raising you."

The two women paused and looked at each other.

"Just look at you. You have turned into a wonderful young woman." Then, almost as if she felt someone's cold hand on her shoulder, she said hurriedly, "They must never know that I told you this as I shall be in trouble, but be safe and well and maybe one day, under different circumstances we can meet again."

Ella was reeling from the information. It was difficult to take in and yet, when the magnitude of the news finally sank in, she was OK with the idea. That explains why I feel so comfortable with her, she thought.

They hugged each other and parted company. Circumstances did not prevail for them ever to see each other again. For a short while Ella felt sad, but from that day forward she had more understanding and compassion for her adopive Mother and she had a better sense of who she was. All of her shyness and insecurities seemed to disperse with the knowledge that she was the product of this beautiful, gentle and kind woman. She no longer needed to live her life wondering why her mother had abandoned her, and she no longer needed to see her adopted mother in a negative light. Maybe she could learn to trust women after all.

Octogenarian sighed. "Sometimes life takes us on different paths and the crossroads we reach do not always take us where we think we want to go, but it does always take us where we need to go."

Amethyst told Patience that turtles were important in the ecology of Inner Wisdom. *Turtles are associated with longevity and are a strong reminder for us to question the hectic pace of our lives. Are we not taking time for ourselves? Are we so busy we cannot really see what is happening around us? The symbol of the turtle was an invitation for blessings from both heaven and earth. (Andrews 2001).*

Prince Charming:

When Ella was 21, she got a job at the local cinema. She used to take the bus home from work every evening and as she was walking from the bus stop to her home one night, something landed on her shoulders.

"Oh! Billy, you scared me. I thought I was being attacked," Ella exclaimed as she realized it was her cat.

Billy had been sitting on the wall waiting for her. From that evening on, every time she came off the bus the cat was there. Ella grew comforted by the consistency of the cat's loyalty and affection.

One day she came home and the cat did not greet her. She was very worried and ran to the house, only to discover that the cat was dead. Someone had poisoned him, her mother told her. She was very distressed. She was convinced it was one of her mother's neighbors, but she could never prove it. Anyway, proof would not bring the cat back. She reaffirmed to herself once again that she should not trust people, especially women. She also told herself that she would never have another cat. She did not want to replace Billy and she did not want to get that close to another animal only to be hurt again. Ella spent the rest of her life not trusting her neighbors and telling herself she did not like animals, especially cats and dogs, but really, deep in her heart she knew that was not true.

One of Ella's many chores was to do the weekly shopping and so every week she found herself at the local butcher shop buying the meat for the week. The son of the butcher was very handsome and was always teasing her. She used to blush at the very thought of having to go into his store and when she stepped off the bus and saw him behind the counter she would think, oh no, there he is again.

"When are you going to give me a free pass for the cinema?" he would ask, joking with her. She could never find the words to answer him and would always flush red and smile quietly. She was always relieved, in a funny kind of way, to get out of the shop. She did find herself thinking about him quite often and she had to admit, as scared as she was, that it was quite exciting to contemplate seeing him again.

One day when she was at work, she saw him coming down the road with his friends. She turned to one of her friends, who was working at the ticket booth that evening.

"See the handsome guy coming down the street. Well, give him and his friends my cinema pass," she said. She then ran inside so that he would not see her.

After she finished work that evening, she walked out to the bus stop as usual and found him waiting for her.

"Thanks for the cinema passes. That was very nice of you," said Bill.

"Oh, you're welcome." Ella blushed and dropped her eyes to the ground.

"Do you mind if I join you for the bus ride home?"

"No, that would be OK," she said nervously. She was very surprised, but secretly pleased.

She wanted the bus ride to go on forever, but of course, it seemed on this particular evening to be all too short. She would not let him walk her all the way to the house, as she felt sure her parents would disapprove of her bringing a man home. She said goodnight to him at the bus stop and hurried home with her heart all aflutter.

That evening was the beginning of a romance that blossomed into eighteen happy years of marriage. The unanswered question in the Cinderella story is whether the Prince and Cinderella really did live happily ever after. Everyone wants to believe they did, but deep down we probably all know they had just as many rocks on the road as the rest of us common mortals.

Marriages in the Village of Illusions were no exception and yet Ella and Bill's marriage was, in many ways, better than most. They lived in the State of Happiness for most of their marriage. They had four children and for the most part everyone got along and had fun together. One of the thorns in the rose bush, however, was the fact that Bill's parents, who owned the local butcher shop and considered themselves middle class and not lower working class, did not approve of their son "marrying down."

"She is not in your social class. Her father is a coal miner and her mother drinks," they would say. "What are you doing? Can't you find a nice girl from your own social group?"

"She is the woman I want to marry and you can't stop me," he had insisted.

They did not stop him, but that did not mean they had to accept her. They made it perfectly clear to her throughout her marriage that she was "not one of them." She tried very hard to be seen in their eyes as a good wife, mother and daughter-in-law, but to no avail. When she was with them, she felt second-class; which, of course, reinforced her feelings of insecurity and inadequacy.

When her first child, a daughter, was born, her mother-in-law softened towards her a little, referring to her now as "the mother of my granddaughter."

Ella was not sure she liked this "promotion," as it felt very patronizing.

Ella and Bill spent many happy years together raising their family. They went to church together every Sunday at Illusions Parish Church.

Since Bill now owned the butcher shop, they were never short of good food and ate meat every day. Each year they would take a four-week vacation to the seaside town of Idealism where they would rent a house for the month. Bill would commute back and forth between Illusions and Idealism, leaving Idealism early Monday morning and returning on Friday evening. Ella and the children spent the week playing on the beach, eating good food, laughing with friends and most of all waiting for Bill to return each Friday evening.

The year Bill turned 47 he suddenly became ill and died three days later. Ella and her four children were devastated. Her children were 18, 17, 8 and 7 years of age when this happened. From that day on Ella was never truly happy. She eventually did remarry, but it never really worked out and when her second husband died of a heart attack, she turned down all other suitors and spent the rest of her life living alone. She actually spent most of her time in the State of Anxiety and the State of Limitations. She remained very distrusting, especially of women, including, on occasions, her daughters and granddaughters. She was increasingly depressed and angry and not much consoled her, except perhaps the presence of her grandchildren and her regular two glasses of scotch every evening. Bill and she had always enjoyed a drink in the evenings. No one was going to stop her and, besides, the doctor said it was good medication for her.

Helen Turnbull, Ph. D.

TURTLE TALK

Reframing reality down at the pond:

Senior Turtle had been looking forward to this story and seemed very excited as he ushered the animals and fish to hurry up and sit down. He put on his professorial look, glanced over at Octogenarian with a knowing smile and began to read. Just as he began to tell the tale, he heard a movement and noticed that Amethyst and Patience had wandered down to the pond and had sat down on a nearby rock to listen. Amethyst did not always join them for their story-telling sessions. This one must be very important. He started again....

When Bill first set eyes on Ella he thought she was the most beautiful woman he had ever seen. He could think of no one else all day. She used to come to his father's store once a week. He was very happy to see her and looked forward to Fridays when he knew she would arrive. He remembered the year she was crowned Queen of Illusions. Even although they were both young at the time, he thought he had probably fallen in love with her on that day.

Bill had a great sense of humor and thought that the best way to engage Ella and get her attention was to joke with her. He used to tease her a lot and make her blush. He liked the way she blushed. Her shy demeanor and humility appealed to him. He asked her one day when she was going to give him a free pass to the movies, as he knew she worked there. He never thought she would since she rushed out of the store, blushing as usual.

Later that week his friends had wanted to go to the movies. Actually, they wanted to go to the other movie theater, but he persuaded them to go to hers. He did not tell them why, of course, as they would never have agreed and they would have teased him for being a sissy. He made up some story about the movies being better at her theater. Thankfully, his friends bought his story and off they went.

The stars were shining for him that evening. As they reached the ticket counter, a woman told him that one of the ticket agents had offered him and his friends Ella's free pass. Wow, she was interested after all. He could not concentrate on the movie for wondering how he was going to see her. After the movie was over, he decided to tell his friends that he would catch the bus home instead of going for a drink with them. He waited anxiously, hoping that he had made the right decision and that she was indeed riding the bus home.

They were married within six months of that evening. His family was delighted to have Ella as an addition to the family. She was the perfect complement to their son. She was bright, attractive, and although she was initially shy, she had a quiet self-confidence and she was an overall asset to their family. She proved to be a terrific wife and mother. When Bill, Ella, and the children visited his parents it was always a fun event and Ella could not remember a time when she had not felt part of their family. For her it was a great blessing to be welcomed into a new family, after her difficult early years. It had not been easy to face being adopted, not knowing her real mother and living with an unreasonably demanding mother.

Ella, now 79, and Bill at 84, celebrated their fifty-eighth wedding anniversary with their extended family. All four of their children had grown up to be fine upstanding citizens of Illusions. There were now five grandchildren and Bill and Ella were laughing as they watched the children playing. One of their granddaughters was running around, pretending to be a Princess.

"Look at me, Gran," she said. "I am a Princess."

"Yes, you are and a beautiful one at that," her grandmother told her. "And you are a handsome Prince," she said, looking over at her only grandson.

Ella and Bill sipped slowly on their customary one glass of

scotch (which Bill had said was all they should allow themselves, at their age). Ella leaned over and patted Bill on the hand. "Do you remember when I was Queen of Illusions?" she asked.

"Do I remember? You look as beautiful today as you did then. To me you are always Queen of Illusions and Queen of my heart." Ella broke into a smile so large that it almost covered her face. Bill then turned to the children and said, "You know, you are the direct descendants of royalty. That is your grandmother's legacy to you."

Everyone laughed and realized how grateful they were to the Queen of Illusions. From small and meager beginnings, she had acquired status and stature and passed it on to all of them.

As Senior Turtle finished his story, he looked up and saw Amethyst walking slowly away. He thought he saw a tear trickling down her face.

Patience and Amethyst were lost in their own memories. Patience finally broke the silence, and turning to Amethyst she said, "I often wonder how my life would have been different if my father had not died when he was 47."

Chapter Six
Controlling Mr. Fixit

*All judgment is relative. How we think about a person
or a thing is dependent on its surrounding context.
(Aronson 1999)*

"The night is yet young, Patience. Shall we tackle another chapter in the book?" asked Amethyst.

"Yes, why not?" replied Patience eagerly. She was beginning to get the hang of this dream. "Lead the way, Amethyst."

Amethyst smiled quietly to herself. Patience had only scratched the surface of the lessons she held within her soul. Amethyst knew that as much ground as they would cover together in this dream, it would not encompass all of the stories that were there to be told. Patience was destined for great things, but she needed to work through the things that were holding her back and tonight was just the beginning.

"What else am I meant to learn?" asked Patience innocently.

"Ah! Patience, what you are meant to learn and what you are willing to learn might be two different things. We shall have to see. The next chapter is called 'Controlling Mr. Fixit.' Let us go and find a nice spot to settle down and we can draw once again on the wisdom of the silver needle with the wise inner eye to be our guide."

Par for the Course:

"Don't do it like that. I thought I told you how to do it. Do it properly," yelled Joe Fixit.

Helen Turnbull, Ph. D.

Justice Fixit lowered his eyes to the ground as his father yelled at him. To say he was used to his father yelling at him was probably an understatement. It seemed that his father did nothing but yell these days. If he was not yelling at him, he was yelling at his younger sister Hope, and most especially, he would yell at his mother.

Justice hated when his father yelled at his mother and his sister. He did not particularly like being yelled at, but he felt, as a boy, that he could handle it better. His mother always looked unhappy and seemed to sulk through the day with her head lowered and her shoulders hunched, trying as hard as she could to either please her husband or stay out of his way. His sister, Hope was an anxious and nervous girl who was always trying to please her father and never seemed to get it right. She cried a lot when she thought he was angry with her.

Joe considered himself a successful businessperson, a good provider and a reliable husband and father. He was in charge of his household, just as he was in charge of his job. He was the Senior Engineering Manager at a large steel mill. He liked to be known as Joe K. His father's name had been Keen Fixit and he was proud of that name. He had a responsible job with quite a large staff of people. He worked long, but not unbearable hours and he considered himself a tough but fair boss. "Tough love, that's what they need," he would be heard to say when referring to the occasions he had been hard on someone at work, especially the women in his department. Once a week he played cards and had a few beers and that was his enjoyment, his "night on the town," as he would say. During the rest of the week, he would stop off at the Local for a beer on his way home, but he would always be home by 7:00 p.m., expecting dinner to be on the table when he arrived.

The Fixits lived in a reasonably nice part of Illusions. Joe K. had been born into a blue-collar family and through his hard work and efforts, he had managed to climb the social ladder and buy himself a house in a nice neighborhood. All of his neighbors were professional people such as doctors and architects. He felt proud that he had managed to establish such a good lifestyle for his family.

"Hi, Joe, how about a round of golf on Sunday?" shouted Steve, one of Joe's neighbors.

Joe was in the front garden, tending to a broken fence at the time.

"No thanks, Steve, Sunday is family time. Now, if you want to play early on Saturday morning, I can do that."

"Let me ask the wife, Joe, maybe that can be arranged."

Joy Fixit was standing at the other end of the garden talking to Steve's wife at the time.

"Huh! Family time indeed! All he does on a Sunday is watch sports on television and fall asleep in front of the T.V. I hope he does play golf on Saturday, it will be a relief to have him out of the house for six hours," she told Rita. Rita smiled in agreement, knowing exactly what she meant.

"He is a good man," she whispered. "It is just that he is like his father." Her voice trailed off wistfully, almost as if she expected Rita to understand what she meant by that.

Joy was a dainty woman with mousy blond hair, hazel eyes and a sad smile. When she spoke she would quite often whisper, a habit she had unconsciously developed as a means of protection from Joe's judgmental ears.

"You know, when you marry someone, Rita, you sort of naively hope you can change them. I always hoped he would not become his father. I cannot stand his father, but fat chance of that. He seems more like him every day."

Rita laughed. "I know what you mean, Joy. I think we might all have the same issue, but perhaps we are becoming our mothers also," she said thoughtfully.

"Oh help! I hope not!" exclaimed Joy as both women laughed aloud.

"Cut out the hilarity over there. You are both having way too much fun," yelled Steve.

"Yeah, what's so funny?" asked Joe, who was always suspicious of what his wife was saying.

"Oh nothing, Joy and I were just having a philosophical discussion," said Rita, at which point both women laughed again.

Later that week an incident occurred that reminded Joy once again of how volatile life was living with Joe.

Joe stormed into the living room and saw her sitting reading.

"Where is my dinner, woman?" he bellowed.

She had told him earlier that she was preparing dinner and they would eat at 7:00 p.m. It was 6:15 now.

Joe was very hungry. He had not eaten enough lunch earlier that day and, while that was not his wife's fault, he nevertheless was feeling very angry with her at that moment. He went into the kitchen, opened the kitchen cupboard and reached for a can of beans.

"Dinner will be ready shortly, Joe, you don't need to do that."

"You and your stubborn ways," he yelled. "You know I like to eat early. You are deliberately trying to upset my life by not having the dinner ready when I am ready to eat," yelled Joe as he slammed his fist on the counter top.

Helen Turnbull, Ph. D.

Joy was upset, not only at the verbal assault but also at the unjust nature of the attack and at the misplaced blame. She left the room in order to avoid a further showdown. Joe threw the can of beans back in the cupboard, picked up his car keys and stormed out of the house. This event was not atypical of the type of misplaced rage that often occurred in their household. She knew he had had a frustrating day at work, but...

Joy Fixit let out a deep and soul-felt sigh. This outburst had taken her a little bit by surprise. Joe had been doing better recently with his temper and his impatience. She figured he would eventually calm down, at least until the next time. She was very tired of bracing herself for all of the "next times" she knew were inevitable.

Life is a Beach:

One Friday afternoon, which happened also to be Joe K.'s fifty-fourth birthday, he decided to take an afternoon off from work and play a round of golf. He called some of his friends to see if they could join him, but at short notice, no one else was available. No problem, he thought, I can play alone. I like my own company.

When he was in the golf shop signing in, a man approached him and said, "Do you mind if I join you?" He was an older man, almost wizardly in his appearance, but

Joe K. did not think much about that especially as he was not very observant.

He had really set his mind on playing by himself, but in the game of golf, it is not good etiquette to refuse to join other players, so Joe K. did the right thing and said, "Of course I don't mind, please join me."

Joe K. teed off first. His drive was long and mostly straight, with a little tail at the end that made his ball land just off the fairway at the 150-yard marker.

His playing partner stood on the tee, addressed the ball and let an enormous drive rip down the fairway. It passed Joe's drive by at least 50 yards. Joe was impressed. Wow, maybe this would not be so bad after all. It did seem that the stranger knew how to play the game.

In the Village of Illusions, it was too hot to play golf by walking the course, as they still liked to do in the Old Country, so Joe and his new friend shared a golf cart together. As they drove to the next tee a butterfly fluttered past, just missing Joe's nose, but he did not notice because he was too intent on getting on with the task to pay attention to anything so apparently insignificant.

THE VILLAGE OF ILLUSIONS

They played the first few holes in silence. After a while, they began to talk. The stranger asked Joe about his work and his family. Joe was happy to tell him.

"I have a really good life, you know. Nice wife, great kids and a responsible job. Actually, when I come to think of it, life is a beach," he said with a smile. The old man raised his eyebrows and smiled knowingly in response.

Joe played the front nine well, even if he did say so himself, and he was feeling pretty pleased about that. No "tomahawks" needed today. When he hit a shot that really displeased him, he would throw his club on the ground so hard that it wedged into the grass like a tomahawk. He was legendary for it and his friends often teased him, calling him Tomahawk Joe.

It was on the back nine that things started to go wrong. In fact, they became so peculiar that you would have thought that he did not know how to play the game. On the 10th hole, he drove his ball out of bounds.

An expletive crossed his mind, but he did not say it aloud since he did not know the stranger well enough to let loose with a sample of his often-colorful language. His companion, as always, drove the ball long and straight as an arrow.

He did not particularly want to lose the ball he had just driven out of bounds, so he went off into the woods to look for it. He liked to use Apex golf balls. They got a lot of distance and he enjoyed their advertising campaign, which showed the golf ball traveling across mountains, oceans, valleys and entire continents. A little far fetched perhaps, but that is how he felt when he hit a good drive.

His companion came with him and they both searched for about three minutes. He knew that under the rules of golf, by which, of course, he always abided, he could only search for five minutes. After about four minutes he came across a large beach ball lying on the ground in just about the location he had calculated his ball would have landed. He pushed it aside, assuming that some children had lost it or left it there.

His companion walked over to the beach ball and said, "I think this is yours, Joe. It has Apex stamped on the top of it and JK initials written all over it."

Joe was flabbergasted. "That is the most preposterous thing I have ever heard," he exclaimed. "It's a golf ball I am looking for, not a freaking beach ball."

The stranger smiled his enigmatic smile and said, "Well, Joe K., you did say life was a beach, did you not?"

Helen Turnbull, Ph. D.

    Joe stared at the man for a long minute and then he sat down on the nearest log to take in what was happening. He had the strangest feeling, as if his world had turned upside down. He felt as if he had lost his golf ball down a ravine and was standing with his head pressed against one of its walls with his feet wedged precariously against the other. He felt quite light-headed at the thought. What happened next made him even dizzier.

THE VILLAGE OF ILLUSIONS

GOLF RAVINE SCENE

"You know, a beach ball is a very interesting thing. It has many different shapes and colors. Different perspectives," the old man said. "If you are looking at it from where you are sitting you will see different things than I can from this side." Suddenly he spun the beach ball in front of Joe, who at this stage was too perplexed even to think. As the ball stopped spinning, it was as if a television screen had opened up in front of him. The stranger might as well have said, "Joe K. Fixit, this is your life," because right there in front of Joe was a "docudrama" of him at work.

He was just finishing a staff meeting, which he remembered from last week. It had been a particularly difficult meeting with many contentious items on the agenda. It was budget time and with the economy being so bad, everyone had to tighten their belts. He watched himself on the beach screen as he yelled at some of his staff for not meeting their budgets. He then turned to the secretary and berated her because his coffee was cold.

At the end of the meeting, as his staff was leaving the room he called after them, "Don't forget to earn your keep today. We're not paying you to goof off, you know." He had been joking, but no one had laughed.

The scene faded and the old man handed him a very large pair of sunglasses. "Would you like to see yourself from the perspective of your staff?"

Joe realized this was more of a rhetorical question, as he did not believe he could have refused to look. He reluctantly and nervously took the glasses.

Some of his staff members were now sitting in the staff coffee lounge, having just left the meeting.

"He is a joke," one of them said. "He thinks he is so big and important, but he's really just an autocratic and overbearing buffoon."

"He talks about having an open door policy and how he offers 'tough love.' Huh! He does not even know that almost everyone fears him. He is so inaccessible and arrogant that no one would dream of asking him for anything. He thinks he has the right answer for everything. He never listens to anyone's ideas and the only opinion he values is his own. There is no such thing as love in his vocabulary. The only love I can think of is that 'there is no love lost' when I think of him."

Joe was crushed. He hung his head and did not know what to say. The old man waited for a few minutes and then he said, "Here is another pair of glasses. Maybe if you look through them you can see some alternatives for how to play the game."

Joe was very willing to get rid of the first pair, so he quickly substituted them. This time he saw a very different picture.

THE VILLAGE OF ILLUSIONS

Instead of driving the meeting aggressively and having it end up in the woods, he was looking much more relaxed and was asking people for their ideas on how they could save money. He was asking questions, waiting for answers, listening and looking very interested in what people had to say. Everyone seemed to be enjoying the meeting and when the secretary got up to get him another cup of coffee, he said, "Don't worry, that's not necessary. The first one was terrific, but I can get my next one myself, thanks."

As the meeting broke up one of his new managers stayed behind and said, "Joe, I just want you to know that since I have joined your department I have felt more empowered than I have in fifteen years. Beyond doubt, you know how to make people feel you trust them to get on and do the job and yet you are always there for us. I truly enjoy working for you and want to thank you for your inspired leadership."

"Which pair of glasses would you like to keep?" The old man asked.

"The ones I am wearing, without a doubt," Joe said, "but I don't know if they quite fit me yet."

"They will, they will," said his companion with a knowing nod. "Let's get back to our game."

The rest of the hole was uneventful. As it was a par 5, Joe managed to bogey it, despite his "out-of-bounds" experience.

The next couple of holes were not his best golf but, overall, he did quite well. It was when they were driving down the fairway of the 13th hole, which was another par 5, that things started to go off the tracks again. Until then he had been persuading himself that the incident on the 10th hole was a figment of his imagination.

He had hit an uncharacteristically enormous drive on the 13th hole and as they were driving down the fairway towards his second shot, he became aware that the golf cart was changing. It was transforming itself into a beach buggy with a striped canvas roof like a deck chair and it had driver's mirrors on either side. It also had a rear-view mirror. Joe felt as if he had been transported into a scene from "Mary Poppins," "The Love Bug," "Chitty Chitty Bang Bang," and "The Prisoner" simultaneously. He half expected a beach ball to come chasing down the fairway after him.

Instead, the old man drew his attention to his left hand driver's mirror. Joe's heart fell into his golf shoes as he realized what he was watching.

"It's all right, Hope, don't cry. He didn't mean it," said Justice, with his arm around his sister trying to console her. The two children were upstairs in Hope's bedroom, where she had rushed after her father had had one of his usual bouts of rage towards her.

Hope was sobbing almost uncontrollably. "I am always in trouble with him. It is not fair; he never lets me go out with my friends. He is always finding a reason why I am wrong. I hate him," she sobbed.

"He *isn't* fair. You know that," said Justice as if acknowledging someone's meanness somehow makes it better.

"I hate him. I wish we had someone else for a father. Anyone would be better than him," Hope cried.

Just at that moment, the bedroom door flew open and there was Joe, larger than life and very threatening. "What is going on here? I thought I told you to go to your bed. I did not tell you to sit there and whine."

Hope tried to wipe her tears, not because she wanted to stop crying, but because she was too afraid to continue for fear it would make him even angrier. Justice lowered his eyes and started to leave the room. As he passed Joe, he turned back and made a face at him, accompanied by a very disrespectful gesture.

Of course, when the incident actually happened Joe had been unaware of that, but now, watching himself in the driver's mirror of his golf cart he saw not only the incident but also the venom that accompanied the gesture.

As the scene faded from view, Joe glanced up, just in time to see that out of the rear-view mirror another scene was fading in. This time Joe's father was standing in the doorway of Joe's bedroom. He was yelling and hurling abuse at him, telling him that he could not go out because he had not completed his schoolwork. Joe, at the age of twelve, was cowering in the corner of his bedroom as his father's tirade continued.

A chip off the old block. People used to say that to him almost as if it was a compliment. His wife was always telling him he was just like his father and he knew she did not mean it in a complimentary way. However, he had never before realized the deep-rooted connections between his childhood and how he now behaved. Joe was not sure how much more of this golf game he could take. He was ready to quit, but the old man was not finished.

"What would it feel like to be your son? What would you do?" asked his playing companion.

Joe stammered a stilted response. "I am not sure, sir, but I am sure I would not be very happy having me as a father." The old man tilted his head almost as if he wanted Joe to keep speaking, so Joe continued, and as he continued, he felt as if even his voice changed, sounding more like his son.

"I hate the fact that Dad shouts at us. He is so foul-tempered that I do not like being around him. I wanted to have a dad just like my best friend

Tommy. His dad spends real time with him. He goes to baseball and football games with him. He builds toy airplanes with him. He works on his Boy Scout projects with him and sometimes goes on camping trips. He even hugs him and tells him he loves him sometimes. Why can't I have a father like that?"

A tear formed at the back of Joe's eyes. He was not sure if he was choking up at the thought that he never had that kind of father, or because his son did not.

As if the old man sensed his despondency and wanted to give him hope, he indicated to Joe to look in the right hand mirror of the cart.

By this time, Joe was beginning to get the picture. He felt sure that the right hand mirror contained the potential for a better relationship with his children. Despite his desire to have that opportunity, he was also scared. Up until a few moments ago, he had not realized that he was not the model father, so he was not exactly feeling confident at the idea that he could become one.

"When your family and colleagues see you are trying to improve, that can make all the difference to their feelings about you."

Joe nodded his head, still feeling ashamed at the impact he had had on his children's lives. He was always telling people at work that they had to pay attention to the difference between intention and impact, but it seemed he had not been paying attention to his own words. No wonder he had no credibility with his staff or his children.

He turned his full attention to the right hand mirror.

Joe was cutting the lawn using his newly acquired power lawn mower. Justice walked towards him. "Hi, Dad, can I join you?"

"Of course," called Joe, "jump on." Justice jumped up beside Joe and the two of them spent a happy 30 minutes racing the lawn mower around the lawn as if they were trying to win a Grand Prix.

When they were finished, Joy brought them cold drinks. "You two look like you've been working hard," she said. "Here are some refreshments."

While they were sitting together in the garden, Justice started talking about his day at school. "You know, Dad, I am really happy I can talk to you. One of my friends, David, his father is such a bully. He never listens to him and David is very unhappy. He says he wishes he had a dad like you. Do you think he could come over and spend the weekend?"

Just at that moment, Hope arrived in the garden. She was laughing and having fun with one of her girlfriends. "Dad, they're doing a career day at our school and I told the teacher that you would speak about engineering. Will you?"

"Of course I will," said Joe, "and yes, Justice, David can spend the night with us. Perhaps I'll give David's father a call and we can get to know each other better," Joe said, turning to Joy with a knowing look.

The scene faded and the old man was holding a five-iron out to Joe. "Why don't you try this club for your next shot?" he asked. By this time, Joe had learned not only did you not ignore the old man's advice, but that the lessons were always relevant. He took the five-iron, hit it beautifully and then watched it soar through the air, land on the green and roll straight into the hole.

"You know, Joe, the rules of golf do not officially recognize the term, but I think scoring a two on a par five might be commonly termed an albatross, don't you?" said the old man with a smile. "Come to think of it, maybe you should leave the albatross here where it belongs and think about the baggage you no longer need to be carrying around your neck."

Joe smiled an uneasy smile. "I think I know what you mean," he said, hoping he was portraying more confidence than he felt.

The 14th hole was relatively uneventful. Although by this time Joe had figured out that there was always calm before the storm and that if his children were the issue on the 13th hole, he was certain he was not getting off this golf course without dealing with the issues with his wife. He had read once that the word GOLF was really an acronym for "**G**entlemen **O**nly **L**adies **F**orbidden," but somehow he knew he was not getting through this day without facing the fact that women could stand on their own two feet in life and on the golf course.

The 15th hole was a short par 4, which meant that Joe would try his hardest to drive the green (which for the non-golfers means that he would try to get his ball on the green in one shot) a feat he rarely accomplished, but one for which he never gave up striving. The idea that he would hit a lay up shot and then ensure a birdie or par was unthinkable to him. He took out his driver and swung as hard as he could. For a while the ball looked like it was going straight and then it took a sharp turn to the left, ending up in the water.

"#@*! Three off the tee." This time he slowed down and tried to swing more carefully. It hit the green and rolled on through, landing in the bunker at the back of the green.

"Beach!" He groaned as he saw the ball roll into the sand.

The old man laughed and said, "Maybe you wanted to go to the beach today after all."

Joe drove the cart up to the green and parked. As he walked towards the sand trap mentally preparing himself to get the ball out of trouble, he found, much to his astonishment, that his wife and a girlfriend were sitting on deckchairs in the sand trap sunbathing and drinking cocktails. He stopped in his tracks. This cannot be happening, he thought. My mind must be playing tricks with me. He started to speak to them and ask them to explain themselves when he realized that they were quite oblivious to him. He was a witness to their conversation, but they did not know he was there. In fact, he could have sworn, had he not known better, that the two women thought they were on the beach as he could hear the ocean waves lapping in the background.

"I can't take it anymore," Joy said to her friend. "He is so aggressive and demanding. Everything has to be his way. Last week he decided to dig up my roses without even discussing it with me. I love my roses, but HE decided they were too much work, so by the time I came home he had thrown them out. I was heartbroken."

"Why don't you leave him? I am sure you and the kids would be much happier without him bullying you all the time. You have not been happy for years," her friend said.

"I've thought about doing that, but it's difficult. We have been together for so long. I used to think we were good friends, but recently ... and the kids, you know ...," her voice trailed off.

"I asked him the other day to help me change a few light bulbs and he went ballistic. If I could have done it myself, I would have. I would never ask him for help if I did not have to. He is so unreasonable and bad tempered. I cannot do anything right for him. He hates the way I wash the dishes; he thinks I do not clean the vegetables properly; I do not cook the chicken well enough; I spend too much money on clothes; and I do not discipline the kids enough. It never ends," she said, finally running out of steam.

"Does he have any redeeming qualities?" her friend asked in a tone that implied she already did not think so.

"Well, yes. Actually, he does." Much to her friend's astonishment, Joy proceeded to defend Joe, telling her how much she valued his integrity, his loyalty and his honesty. "Sometimes he shows a tough exterior but he is really soft underneath. I would trust him with my life and I know he would never let me down. He IS by best friend." Sensing the incongruity of these remarks she added, "I guess you're wondering how he can be both of these things; but he is."

Her friend smiled the smile of resignation that close women friends understand. She knew that Joy was not going to leave Joe, despite his boorish behavior. On some level, she was tired of hearing the same old complaints from Joy and yet she wanted to support her friend in whatever she wanted to do with her life. If she really loved this man, then who was she to talk her out of it? After all, she did not exactly have her life together either. Who did?

Just as Joe was thinking he had seen about all he could take, the two women started to laugh and Joy's friend said, "How do you think Joe would cope if he was a woman?"

"Hah!" laughed Joy, what a great thought. "Maybe we could make him a woman for a day. I will pretend to be Joe! What do you think?" She jumped up to her feet and started mimicking Joe. "Where's my dinner? What do you mean it is not ready? What have you been doing all day?"

Joy's friend got in the spirit immediately and jumped to her feet, lowered her eyes and looked awkward and said, "Sorry, Joe, I went to visit one of my friends this afternoon and I haven't had time..."

"Haven't had time, woman? What are you saying? Your job is to look after me, not waste time with your friends. I expect my dinner on the table at 7:00 p.m.," Joy bellowed.

Both friends dissolved in laughter. Joe did not like what he saw. He was torn between anger at watching his wife mimicking him and the fact that she was talking to her friends about him. He did not like the fact that she talked to her women friends and yet he knew in his heart that if he had treated her better over the years there would be no story to tell about his bad behavior.

He did love her very much. She was his best friend. He thought she knew that. That should have been enough for her, but apparently, it was not. He knew he needed to treat her more respectfully. The blanket of superiority, which he wore like an invisible cape over his attitude towards women, always leaked out in the way he treated them. He pretended to hear what she said, but the truth was that women's voices, including hers, had no credibility with him. Apparently, she could see it. Suddenly he felt like the Emperor with no clothes. Perhaps it was time to change his wardrobe.

GOLF COURSE / BEACH BALL

A Hole-in-One:

The 17th hole was a par 3 and much to Joe's amazement, he had a hole-in-one. He turned around to celebrate with his newfound friend and discovered to his consternation that the old man was nowhere in sight. He had gone, just vanished. There was no one to prove it to, no one with whom to celebrate, no one to validate his hole-in-one. For a moment, Joe was annoyed and then he laughed and realized that his wise old friend was probably telling him that he did not need him now. He was on his own. He was probably also teaching him one last lesson and that was the lesson of humility. He could tell people he had a hole-in-one, but he sure could not brag about it. Well, that was OK, after the eventful day he had had, a hole-in-one was probably the least of his worries.

A moment later, the old man reappeared from the woods at the side of the 17th tee. "I am sorry," he said, "I had to take care of some business; hope I didn't miss anything."

By this time Joe had recovered his decorum and with pragmatic resignation said, "No, nothing. It's your turn to tee off."

As Joe and his companion stood waiting on the 18th tee, he noticed a morning dove sitting on the bush next to the tee. He was not sure why, but he felt some connection with it. He shrugged his shoulders, almost as if he were talking to himself. Ridiculous, he thought. I cannot possibly believe I have a relationship with that bird. I must have gone soft in the head. Then again, it had been a very strange day indeed and not one he would forget in a hurry.

The 18th hole was beautiful. In fact, it should have been the signature hole for the golf course. It had water all the way down the right hand side of the fairway with beautiful palm trees and oak trees surrounding the pond. The birds and animals that lived on the pond were always present and even when you were playing badly you could enjoy taking in the glorious signs of nature at work. That was not something Joe usually took the time to do, but somehow today he seemed to be noticing the beauty around him.

As the final putt clattered into the hole, Joe turned to shake hands with his playing partner, another customary politeness in the world of golf.

The old man shook his hand vigorously and said, "Thank you, Joe K. I enjoyed taking this part of the journey with you. Here is your scorecard." He handed Joe his scorecard and said he must be off as he had other people to meet. After he left, Joe glanced down at the card in his hand and much to his amazement, it was not his golf score, but rather the scores that significant people had given him to reflect their experience of him. It seemed that the front nine was how they felt about him today and the back nine was his potential.

Scorecard: Actual and Potential - Joe K. Fixit

Handicap: Control issues, arrogance and dreadful temper

FRONT NINE:

Actual:	Positives	Negatives	Mixed	Other	Overall
Joy	45	35	10	10	100
Hope	30	70			100
Justice	20	70	10		100

BACK NINE:

Potential: A gentleman, considerate of others, mature, good listener, even-tempered and manages his emotions

	Positives	Negatives	Mixed	Other	Overall
Joy	80	20			100
Hope	65	15	10	10	100
Justice	60	25	10	5	100

(Bentz 1989)

Back at the Island State of Inner Wisdom, Amethyst was tending her rose garden when the morning dove and the butterfly returned, reporting to her that Joe Fixit had had a very meaningful round of golf. Amethyst smiled. She had always believed that golf mirrors life. She remembered the expression that said "a bad day on the golf course is better than a good day at work." Amethyst thought that the morning dove and the butterfly had had a good day on the golf course and that perhaps Joe would now know what a good day at work and home could look like. Perhaps if he used his energies more wisely his golf might also improve, she mused.

When Joe got to the Clubhouse he ordered what he told himself was much-needed refreshment. He was sitting quietly, reflecting on his experience, when a young man came in and said, "Great hole-in-one you had, sir. Congratulations. I saw you from the practice area."

Joe laughed. Practice, he thought. That is just what I need; practice. "Thank you, young man. That is very good advice," he said with a smile.

Patience sighed as she listened to Joe reflecting on his behavior.

"Someone once told me, Amethyst, that we have 86,400 seconds in every day of our life and I am not sure that I have always used them wisely."

"What are you saying, Patience?" "I suspect that I have spent way too many hours fretting about the men in my life; what they thought about me, whether they loved me, why they were angry at me, why they were unkind to me, why they were not talking to me, why they did not want to be with me, why they were not doing what I wanted or needed, etc. etc. Gosh, the list is endless. I used to take up their hobbies just to be with them, even when I did not enjoy it. If only I could take back all the precious seconds I have squandered away. Sometimes it was just bosses or co-workers that made me feel bad. Why have I given away so much of my power?"

"These are pretty deep thoughts, Patience. What is it about Joe's story that makes you raise so many questions about yourself?" asked Amethyst.

Patience thought about the question for some time as silence descended between the two women.

"Oh, it is too long a story for this dream. Perhaps the thing that makes me most sad is that years of being intimidated by aggressive behavior have not only made me protective and defensive, it has also made *me* intimidating, and aggressive. I am so well defended today I doubt if anyone could get close to me. I feel as if I have lost my sweetness and I am not sure I can ever recover the almost naive innocence I used to feel. I used to like myself more than I do today," said Patience wistfully.

"The central core of who you are is always there, Patience. Your soul knows who you are. You have allowed events in your life to block out the essence of who you are. The pilgrimage we all take must ultimately lead us back to ourselves. It may have taken years to get to where you are today, but it may only take a moment of enlightened awareness for you to decide you no longer wish to hold on so tight to that which no longer serves you. If there are, in fact, behaviors that are detrimental, or people that are detrimental to your well-being, then perhaps it is time to let them go. It is possible to love yourself again."

Patience sighed, thinking to herself that while that sounded wonderful it was probably more difficult than it seemed.

"Come on, Patience, let us go on with your journey. It is time to find another chapter, to continue unraveling the old patterns so that you can begin weaving new ones," said Amethyst.

Chapter Seven
Mrs. Baker's Dilemma

There are undoubtedly limits to how much a person can change over the course of a life, and to how many different selves can inhabit a single body or mind at any one time, but we don't know what these limits are. (Anderson 1997)

Alice Baker lived at 23 Main Street in the Village of Illusions, where she had lived for forty years. She was happily married to Bob Baker and they had two grown children and three grandchildren. In July they would be celebrating forty years together. She considered herself extremely fortunate having such a wonderful husband. She also had what she described as a brilliant social life with lots of good friends. Whenever her friends needed anything, she was always there for them. Everyone who knew her said she had a very good heart. She knew they said that and liked the idea of being valued in that way. She had a breathtaking capacity for being spontaneously generous to people. She loved to cook and bake, she excelled at hosting dinner parties, and she really enjoyed having her friends around her and looked forward to any opportunity to spend time with them.

Alice Baker believed that in addition to living in the State of Reality she spent most of her time in the State of Happiness.

"I am a cheerful person and I don't like being around negative people." She was also very fond of saying, "You can depend on me for anything."

Despite her bubbly and gregarious exterior, there were occasions when she was not very happy and in fact could get quite emotional and anxious. She worried constantly about what people thought of her and today was no exception. She was just wrapping up a long telephone conversation with Sheila.

"I must run also, Sheila. I have friends coming for dinner tonight and I need to get busy cooking. I am making my favorite chicken recipe and I know they are going to love it. Before I hang up, though, what did you think of Laura not inviting us to her party? We have never done anything to her. Why would she not include us? I don't think she likes me. Well I don't care anyway; I am too busy to care. It's her loss really. I was thinking of not inviting them to my party. They are not really friends. What do you think?"

"Oh, I don't think she meant anything by it. After all we are a big group and everyone can't be included in every event," Sheila told her friend, hoping that she sounded convincing. Sheila knew that Laura thought Alice did not really like her, but she figured that there was no purpose in telling her that. Why hurt her feelings?

"She doesn't play cards with us anymore; thinks she is too good for us," said Alice in a mocking superior tone.

"I had heard that she was not playing cards with your group anymore."

"Huh, I don't care. She's kind of weird anyway, don't you think? You never know what personality is going to show up," Alice continued.

"It was good to talk with you, but I must run," said Sheila.

Alice wore her heart on her sleeve and got her feelings hurt quite often.

Bob Baker was quite often emotionally exhausted from trying to figure out how to console her. Every day there was another drama. In addition to feeling victimized and hurt all the time she did not know how to say no to people and worried unnecessarily about what other people thought of her.

"Why do you try so hard to be liked by people who are treating you badly? You spend most of your time taking care of others and not enough time taking care of yourself," said Bob in a fit of frustration. "You go on and on about how they treat you and then you end up apologizing to them for your behavior! I don't get it!"

He had just spent twenty minutes listening to Alice complaining about how she had been treated by one of the ladies at the Tennis Club and he was once again out of words to comfort her. Alice had so many issues of rejection that it could be quite tiring trying to calm her. He felt upset when he knew she was hurt, but he was also fatigued and out of options to get her to see that some of the drama she created was self induced.

THE VILLAGE OF ILLUSIONS

Alice's head was spinning as she played repeatedly in her mind her version of the latest drama. Over the years, she had come across people who did not always appreciate her kindness and she would be so hurt at what she perceived to be their rejection of her that she would let her head run away with her heart, making up a story of such intensity against herself. She was the queen of rhetorical statements and often left people feeling she had asked them a question and answered it herself before they had time to draw a breath.

One day when she was attending the Village monthly meeting, she spoke out on behalf of some of the other citizens. She had been feeling quite upset for some time that in her opinion, a particular group of people were being treated unfairly by the Village Council and felt it was time to speak up.

"Lord Mayor, Council members, I have come here today to protest at the unfair and inequitable treatment that the people at the bottom of the village receive. Don't you think it is time that those of us who live at the top of the village, and especially the owners of this village started paying more attention to the needs of others? These poor people need our help and I, for one, am outraged and appalled that we are so oblivious to their plight."

Alice was feeling quite smug as she sat down. She had made what she felt was an impassioned speech, pointing out the inequities and urging the Council to consider the matter. Suddenly a woman stood up and began to speak in a very loud tone.

"Who do you think you are coming in here and speaking for us. What do you know about living at the bottom of the village. You people are all the same. Self righteous do-gooder liberals. You have never been near the bottom of the village and neither have half the people in this room," the woman bellowed.

Alice was in shock. She had thought she was helping and it seemed this woman did not appreciate her help. How ungrateful. She was momentarily stunned and could not think of anything to say. While she was gathering herself another woman stood up.

"Yes, who do you think you are! You are the one who needs fixing, not us! Have you looked at your own lifestyle? So shallow and superficial with your fancy little dinner parties. The truth is you all don't even like each other. At least down at the bottom of the village we have a sense of community and togetherness. We stick together, we actually say hello to one another. You all walk past each other with your noses in the air," the loud woman continued.

This comment was followed by appreciative laughter from the audience.

Alice picked up her purse and slid quietly out of the meeting room. Instead of creating the outcome and the conversation she had hoped for, she found herself chastised by some of the very citizens she thought she was defending. She was very taken aback at their reaction. She left the meeting feeling hurt, rejected, humiliated and indignant.

"Well, I am never going to speak up and help anyone again," she told herself as she walked quickly to her car. She would go home and tell Bob what had happened to her and he would console her. She reflected that she did not always appreciate how much she depended on Bob to be there to support and protect her.

Facing Reality:

A butterfly fluttered past and a morning dove landed on the tree next to where Alice Baker was sitting, just as she was about to tell Sheila how insensitive the people at the bottom of the village had been. She hesitated for a moment, wondering if she should really be talking about people like that. Then disregarding the thought, she proceeded to tell her story. She often needed just to share her feelings of hurt and rejection. She was an extrovert and it was always easier to talk through what she was feeling.

"You know, Sheila, I don't always like myself when I talk badly about people. I worry that others might think I share too much and maybe I am gossiping, but I must tell you what happened at the village meeting today. I cannot believe how ungrateful these people were. I went there to help them and they turned on me. It was so rude! I will never stick my neck out for anyone again," protested Alice.

Sheila listened in amazement, shaking her head and wondering what the other side of the story was. What would the people at the bottom of the village have to say about this event? She knew that there would be more than one side to the story, but in the meantime, she set about comforting her inconsolable friend.

When Bob Baker came home that evening, Alice immediately rounded on him.

"Oh Alice, please don't start in on me as soon as I walk through the door, give me a few minutes to rest and get myself a beer."

Quite often Bob needed a few beers just to get through the evening.

Alice was in full flight and was not going to be stopped, not even for Bob's beer.

THE VILLAGE OF ILLUSIONS

"I cannot believe how rude these people were today and the Mayor and the Council members did not even stop them. You know, we should not vote for them next election, Bob. They should all be fired. And as for the bottom of the village, it will be a long, cold day before I decide to help them again," thundered Alice.

"Are you listening to me, Bob?"

Bob sighed as he tried to play down the incident.

"Yes, Alice, I am listening to you. You should not take these things so seriously. First of all you probably should not have interfered. Why did you go there and appoint yourself to be their spokesperson anyway? I am sure they meant no harm and it was not a personal attack on you. Anyway, why are you giving these women so much power over you? They don't really matter in the big picture. We have a good life here, with good friends," said Bob, hoping he was being helpful.

Alice was furious at him for not understanding.

"That is so typical of you, Bob, to take other people's side and not hear mine" she screeched. "Not only am I attacked at the meeting, but now I look for sympathy with my own husband and you take their side." She stomped out of the room and Bob reached for another beer. He walked quietly over to his favorite chair and switched on the television. It was a drama a day with Alice.

While she was making dinner later that evening, Alice's mind was whirling with the day's events. They were surprising thoughts, not the kind of questions she was used to asking herself. She was having second thoughts. Was she being reasonable to expect everyone at the meeting to agree with her opinions? Had she over-reacted? Had she misread the situation? Had she perhaps made her case too strongly? Should she have spoken up at all? Perhaps it was not her job or her business to have intervened in that way. Was it bad timing on her part? Maybe it was not that important in the bigger picture. Perhaps they thought she was being opinionated and not as helpful as she thought she was. Perhaps she was, but how could she fix that now? She considered not attending any more meetings. It would be a long time before they saw her at another meeting, she told herself with conviction. After all, it would be their loss. This was not the first time she had found herself in this kind of fix. Perhaps there was a pattern here. Was it worth looking at the possibility that she was the central player in her own dramas? Alice Baker pondered that thought for quite a long time.

Woody, Amethyst's trusty morning dove friend, felt happy. Mrs. Baker was questioning her own behavior. He knew that he had delivered his message safely, just as Amethyst had asked him to do. It was important for people to look inside for answers, to listen to their inner wisdom and to examine their own behavior and not just the behaviors of others. What Mrs. Baker did with these thoughts now was entirely up to her.

Mr. Baker, in the meantime, had taken himself out for a walk. He thought perhaps he would head in the direction of his local and partake of a few more beers. On his way there he had to walk past a canal. He had taken this walk many times and was familiar with the scenery and the route. On this particular day his mind was wandering as he pondered over his wife's latest drama. He was asking himself over and over what he could possibly do to get her to stop being so upset. She seemed to become dramatic over nothing, or at least that is how it seemed to him. Suddenly he heard a voice.

"I bet you feel like going to the State of Despair," the voice said.

Mr. Baker was startled. He looked all around and could not see where the voice was coming from. He could have sworn it was coming out of the ground. He looked down at his feet and right there in front of him was a very large turtle.

"How do you know how I feel? You are right on the money though, Mr. Turtle."

Yikes, that beer I drank at home must have been stronger than I realized, thought Mr. Baker. I am hallucinating and talking to a turtle!

"Actually, my name is Octogenarian," said the turtle

"Oh, nice to meet you, Octogenarian," said Mr. Baker with a wry smile.

"Sometimes I feel like I am being so impatient and short tempered with her, but I honestly don't know what to do to stop her from getting so involved and getting hurt. I get very frustrated as I watch these tumultuous events unfold. They seem like storms in a teacup to me, and honestly, as much as I love her, she is the ultimate drama queen."

"Have you thought about asking her to look at that? Perhaps you might suggest that you see a pattern and she might benefit from reflecting on what drives her drama queen behaviors."

"Oh! You are joking, right. She would kill me if I called her a drama queen, or even got close to suggesting it. Honestly, we are lucky; we have our health and we have many good friends and yet she is always so down on herself and other people. She is so negative these days. She worries about being rejected and then lo and behold, she gets rejected! She wears her heart on her sleeve and that is why she always feels hurt. Perhaps that is why I fell in love with her, because she is so open and loving. I have spent many years shoring up her emotional insecurities, but I guess that is what you do when you love someone."

GETTING UNSTUCK

"Let me share a story with you. Perhaps it will help," said Octogenarian.

Woody is a morning dove who lives on a very beautiful island. One day Woody's cousin, Flapper, found himself stuck in a swimming pool. He was not quite sure how he had ended up there, but in order to stop his tail feathers from getting too wet, he had skipped onto the first piece of solid matter he could find, only to discover it was a swimming pool vacuum cleaner. He got one of his claws caught in the piping and could not move. The pool cleaner was vibrating quite rapidly as it moved around the pool and Flapper was taken for a very reluctant and jarring ride. Flapper stayed there for quite a long time. The experience was so overwhelming that he just sat there, becoming more scared by the minute. Eventually the woman and man of the house came home and saw his plight. The woman came out and rescued him. He was not sure at first what to do, but he was so scared he could not fly away anyway, so he just stood there shaking as she pulled the vacuum cord onto dry land. Eventually he stepped off the plastic and onto the pool deck and just sat helplessly beside the kind woman. Then the man of the house came over to help. Flapper knew that they wanted to help him and he thought to himself that they were very good people to be so concerned, but he did not know what to do. They seemed so large and imposing, making him nervous again, so he ran quickly into the nearest bush to hide.

He stayed in the bushes for hours. The nice woman and man came over to talk to him a few times, but he did not come out of hiding. Long after they had left for the evening he finally decided to venture out, realizing that he would need to help himself to get back on track and that not only was no one else going to do it for him, but that no one else could. Staying under the bush and looking like a wounded bird was probably a dangerous option. A cat could have found him. It was time to fly home, where his mother reminded him not to play in swimming pools ever again.

"I think perhaps Flapper's tale is also typical of human beings, getting themselves stuck, not asking for help, being offered help, but not being able to accept it, and then finally working out that they had better take care of themselves," said Octogenarian in a very professorial tone of voice.

Mr. Baker stood there shaking his head. He was still mesmerized at the thought that he was listening to a turtle, but his good manners would not allow him to be rude. He thanked the turtle for his story, bid him good day and continued on his journey, wondering as he went what he needed to do to take better care of himself. Perhaps he would go and have a beer and think about that.

In the meantime, Amethyst and Patience were sitting on the bench at Inner Wisdom Avenue. Woody and Flapper suddenly flew across their paths.

"Gosh, you two are in a hurry today."

"Oh, hello, Amethyst," said Woody. "Sorry, we did not mean to startle you. We were just talking about Mrs. Baker. She seems so anxious. A lot of people seem to spend much of their lives feeling anxious."

Amethyst thought perhaps this was an ideal time to check in with Patience.

"So, Patience, how are you feeling? Are you enjoying the story you selected?" asked Amethyst.

Patience thought for a few moments and then said, "I am not sure if 'enjoying' is the best word to describe it. I am most definitely finding it enlightening, and perhaps it does make me feel a little anxious."

"What are you feeling anxious about?" asked Amethyst.

"When I first started listening to Mrs. Baker's dilemma, I thought to myself, I know people like that! I have friends who fit that description, but the more I listened the more I realized that many of Mrs. Baker's traits and characteristics are also mine. Truthfully, Amethyst, I have spent lots of time in the State of People Pleasing. I am the quintessential drama queen and I live almost permanently in the State of Anxiety, the State of Insecurity and the State of Neediness. In fact, I would say that the State of Rejection is also one of my regular haunts." Patience was silent for a moment as she let the enormity of what she was saying sink in. She then added, "I have spent many years worrying about what other people thought of me and trying to please them, quite often at my own expense. I want to be accepted, I want to be liked and I am always afraid to let my own feelings come to the surface, especially if it means saying no to someone and then risking their rejection of me."

"Are you still doing these things today?" asked Amethyst.

"Yes, but I think the older I get the less I am willing to do that, but I still worry about it. So perhaps I spend more time in the State of Anxiety than I should. One of my issues today, which again is similar to Mrs. Baker, is that I always want to jump in and defend other people, so I have trouble managing my mouth sometimes. I often speak up and then wish I had kept quiet. I spend a lot of anxious time worrying about what I should say, what I have said and what makes me remain silent. Then, to top it off, worrying about what people think of me because I said it in the first place! Appropriateness is a huge issue for me. I am always asking myself, 'Am I being appropriate?' whatever that means," said Patience.

"Then it is a good thing that we are headed to the State of Anxiety next," Amethyst said with a smile, at the same time beckoning to Patience to return to the story.

The State of Anxiety:

Anxiety was a very chaotic State. It was very windy there and, in fact, it was so windy that people felt they had to keep moving in order to synchronize themselves with the constant movement. There was a sense of swirling energy all around. Suddenly, as if out of nowhere, a man appeared, dressed in a very colorful suit and carrying a very important-looking briefcase. His arms were flying in all directions.

"I'm late," he cried by way of explanation, as he bumped into a woman carrying a large package. He sounded like a twenty-first-century version of the Mad Hatter in Alice in Wonderland, thought the woman. (Carroll 1960)

"Why do people always bump into me?" asked Mrs. Saddled. She carried on walking, grumbling to herself and eventually came to a park bench where she decided to rest for a while. She was feeling very burdened down by life lately and this man's rude behavior was just another example of how she felt she was constantly being victimized. She carefully put down her package and as she did so, she noticed some children playing in the distance.

I hope they do not come near me, she thought. I do not like children. They are usually noisy and rowdy and they may damage my package. Oh dear, can't a person just be allowed to rest peacefully without having to worry about such things? Well, I will just rest for a short while and then my package and I will be on our way.

With the morning sun beating down, Mrs. Saddled quickly fell asleep. She was a small, rotund woman who had a perpetually anxious look on her face. If one did not know better they would have sworn that she had been born frowning. As she slept, she started to snore quietly. The children playing nearby heard the noise and came closer to see what was happening, but they never disturbed her. It was a good thing, too, as Mrs. Saddled would not have wanted to think of herself as someone who snored. That would be extremely unladylike and she would have been embarrassed if someone had told her. She liked to think of herself as perfect, so the idea that anyone would suggest that she was not would not have been palatable.

Meanwhile, Mr. Harrowed, who had bumped into her earlier, was still rushing. He was not sure what he was rushing to, but he did know for sure that he was late. It seemed that he had so much to do these days and he was so important that all he could do was rush from place to place, hardly even stopping for breath. Mr. Harrowed, unlike Mrs. Saddled, was tall and angular, almost like a lanky matchstick man. He hardly ever smiled, probably because his face always looked like it was going through the sound barrier, with his skin pressed back taut against his bony features. His arms and legs were very long and gangly and he looked like a giant giraffe.

As he turned the next corner he bumped into a hare so large that it stopped him in his tracks. The hare was sporting a kilt and a Tam O'Shanter and spoke with a distinctly Scottish accent! For most people that would have seemed like an extraordinary event, but Mr. Harrowed was so busy rushing that he did not stop to take in the bizarre nature of the situation. As far as he was concerned, all he knew was that someone had had the audacity to stop him in his tracks.

"Where are you rushing to, sir?" asked the hare politely.

"I'm not really sure," said Mr. Harrowed, "but I know it's important."

The hare considered this response for a minute and then invited the man to stop and have some munchies with him.

Well, it could not really hurt to take a break. After all, even on his busy schedule there was time for a pit stop.

THE VILLAGE OF ILLUSIONS

The hare led him into a room that looked like a dining room. There was a table with ten very grand chairs and on the wall, there were two pictures, hanging closely together. Each frame showed half of a very pretty park avenue, lined with trees. A low park wall that was architecturally pleasing surrounded a small lily pond. Both sides of the painting were perfectly symmetrical and together they made a very inviting scene.

"What is this?" asked Mr. Harrowed impatiently. "I thought we were going for refreshments? There are no snacks here. I don't have time to be messing around."

Helen Turnbull, Ph. D.

MIRROR IMAGE PARK

"We ARE going for Afternoon Tea," said the hare. "Allow me to introduce you to Mirror Image Park. Which side of the park appeals to you most?"

"What are you talking about?"

"Pick one, right or left," said the hare impatiently in a brusque guttural tone.

Mr. Harrowed was so startled by the hare's obvious annoyance that he quickly, selected the right side. Before he knew it, he found himself whisked into the picture, and was walking down the right side of Mirror Image Park Avenue alongside the Highland hare.

"Where are you taking me?" Mr. Harrowed asked. "I am in a hurry, you know."

"Yes, yes, I know that, but I want to introduce you to some of my friends before you rush off," answered the hare with a mischievous smile.

The hare or rabbit can show you how to recognize the signs around you and to become more conscious of the tides of movement within your life. The hare also has a wonderful ability for defensive tactics. It is always planning escape routes and has the capacity to freeze, not be noticed, and then to take off at great speed. (Andrews 2001).

Back on the park bench, Mrs. Saddled had begun to dream. She found herself standing in a dining room, next to what looked like two pictures of a pretty park avenue. She saw movement on the right side of the avenue and looked more closely through the glinting of the sun. There was a fawn beckoning her to come closer. *When fawn or deer show up in your life it is time to be gentle with yourself and others. A new innocence and freshness is about to be awakened and there is the enticing lure of new adventures. (Andrews 2001).*

Before she knew it, she was following the fawn down the avenue towards what looked like a large atrium. Outside the atrium was a table with a number of people sitting there having tea. The fawn led her over to the table and a hare invited her to sit down.

"Oh my goodness, what is she doing here?" said Mr. Harrowed.

"There is that dreadful man who had the audacity to bump into me earlier today and knock down my package," echoed Mrs. Saddled.

Suddenly she remembered that she had left her package behind and began to panic. The fawn and the hare quickly reassured her that her package was OK and it would be there when she returned, if she still wanted it.

The scene in front of her was a remarkable sight. There was a very large table with some of the grandest chairs she had ever seen. They had very tall backs and olive green fabric with a nice leaf pattern of red and burnt umber. They were very pleasing to the eye and reminded her of autumn. Fortunately, there were four empty chairs. Mrs. Saddled took one of them, the fawn, the hare and that dreadful man took the other three. The table was set for afternoon tea with the biggest teapot and coffee pots she had ever seen. There was a large plate of cakes on the middle of the table and at the far end of the table, another large plate of scones with cream and preserves. It all looked very tempting.

The other people at the table did not look as pleased as she did. In fact, they looked quite unhappy.

The hare stood up and brought the party to order. He announced in a grand tone, "Today we have two visitors, so why don't we all introduce ourselves and then we will hear from our guests."

Everyone began to speak at once, causing a hullabaloo. "One at a time please," insisted the hare. "I know you are anxious, but let's remember our manners."

A hush fell over the group and from the far end of the table someone began to speak. "Welcome to the State of Anxiety and to our monthly Refreshment meeting. We are all in quite a state here and I am Miserable."

Miserable, thought Mr. Harrowed and Mrs. Saddled simultaneously. They thought people were supposed to be introducing themselves, not describing how they were feeling.

As if reading their minds, the fawn leaned over and reassured them that that was indeed his name. "He is Miserable, by name and by actions."

Oh dear, thought Mrs. Saddled, that is very sad.

One at a time, everyone seated at the table offered their welcome and gave their name.

"I am Ms. Despair."

"I am Mr. Helpless."

"I am Mrs. Chronically Lonely."

In addition, Mr. Chaotic, Mrs. Very Anxious, and Mr. Constantly Victimized were present.

Ms. Co-Dependent and Mr. Counter-Dependent were too busy to notice the new arrivals as they were arguing at the other end of the table, intent on establishing once and for all, which one of them was more important.

The only one at the table who seemed to be smiling suddenly jumped up, grabbed a bunch of daffodils from the table, and ran over to them. As she handed them each some flowers she put her hands on their arms and said, "And I am Mrs. People-Pleaser and I am awfully glad you are here. Welcome, welcome, welcome."

"Well, now it is your turn," said the hare. "Introduce yourselves."

Mr. Harrowed and Mrs. Saddled, who found themselves becoming fast friends, or perhaps just bonding out of necessity, shot each other an anxious glance across the table.

"What does this mean? What should we do?" Mrs. Saddled dropped her eyes to the floor and Mr. Harrowed took that as a sign that he should go first. Anyway, he was in a rush and wanted to get this over with, and as a man he was used to asserting his authority and speaking first.

Mr. Harrowed drew a deep breath and put on his most business-like tone, a tone he felt was in keeping with the importance of his leather briefcase. "I am Mr. Harrowed and I am very surprised to be here. I think you all seem very unhappy, with the possible exception of Mrs. People-Pleaser, and in my opinion you should all just cheer up. After all, it is a beautiful day. I also notice that most of your names seem quite depressing and your personalities seem to match your names. Perhaps you should consider changing your names?"

A groan reverberated around the table, accompanied by a lot of shaking of heads, knowing looks and rubbing of chins. Just like a man to act in such an entitled manner. Someone muttered "Huh! Look who is talking! Mr. Harrowed, indeed!"

"Now, now," said the fawn, "let's not be judgmental, or at least let's hold our judgments. It is time to hear from our second guest."

By this time, Mrs. Saddled was feeling very nervous and anxious. She had spent most of her life feeling burdened with one thing or another. This task of introducing herself to these rather scary and depressing people just made her feel even more victimized. Why me? I wish I could wake up now. However, she took a deep breath and began to speak.

"I am Mrs. Saddled and I think this is a dream, no, maybe even a nightmare. You all seem very strange to me. I am considerably inconvenienced by being here. I don't really want any of your refreshments and I would just like to wake up, get back to my package and be on my way."

"Where would you be going in such a hurry?" chimed Mr. Helpless, who had a green pointed hat, blushing red cheeks and an Irish accent.

"Back to the park bench to collect my package," Mrs. Saddled retorted.

"She is quite ungrateful and rude, is she not?" declared Mr. Constantly Victimized. The group nodded in agreement.

"You are rejecting our hospitality and we are feeling most anxious about that," they said in unison. Mrs. Saddled became very flustered. She was beginning to think it was best not to make any more fuss when

Mr. Harrowed, sensing that the atmosphere was turning tense, reached over and touched Mrs. Saddled on the arm and said, "Perhaps it would be best if you sat down for now."

Mrs. Saddled decided to take Mr. Harrowed's advice and slid quietly back into her very large chair. Mrs. People-Pleaser clapped her hands together in glee and said, "Oh great, now let's have refreshments."

In most polite societies, it is customary to make conversation when breaking bread with other people. Despite the anxious nature of their meeting, none of its members had lost their manners and people began to speak and listen to each other. Ms. Co-Dependent had decided to get in on the action and she came over and sat next to Mrs. Saddled. Leaning over in a conspiratorial tone she said, "What is in your package, anyway? What makes it so important?"

Mrs. Saddled was startled by the question. For one thing, no one had ever asked that before and, for another, she really did not know the answer. "You know, I am not sure. It is just that I have been carrying it around for so long that I would not know what to do without it."

"Does it feel like a burden?" asked Ms. Co-Dependent.

"Well, yes, come to think of it, it does. I had never thought about it like that, but it does, yes, it does, indeed it does feel like a burden."

"Is it your package, or are you carrying it for someone else?" asked Ms. Co-dependent, quickly adding, "Other people are like that, you know. They will land you with their packages and let you carry them. I know I have many stories I could tell you about that. Perhaps you are holding on to this package too tightly?"

Mr. Counter-Dependent butted into the discussion at this point.

"Ah! Do not let anyone tell you what to do. If you want to keep carrying your package for the rest of your life, just you go right ahead," he said with an air of defiance in his tone.

Mrs. Saddled was beginning to feel very defensive about her package. After all, it did not really matter if it began life as someone else's package; it was hers now. She had carried it for so long she did not really know what life would be like without it. It gave her a sense of importance and more notably, it gave her a justifiable reason to complain when she felt life was getting her down, which was quite often, if the truth were told.

"I think perhaps you should take Mr. Harrowed's advice and change your name and then perhaps you will not be saddled with other people's packages," said Ms. Co-dependent with the pragmatism and pathos of someone who had already been there.

While Mrs. Saddled was pondering this prospect, Mr. Harrowed was having his own version of Tea and Sympathy.

THE VILLAGE OF ILLUSIONS

"You know, I kind of like rushing around," said Highland Hare. "It makes me feel important. In fact, I see people moving out of my way all the time, because they realize how important I am." He puffed out his chest as he spoke. That is, as much as a hare is capable of puffing out his chest.

There was a loud choking sound from the other end of the table. A man with a long twisted face, a lot of wrinkles, a very pukka English accent and a large bowler hat, which was almost too big for his head, guffawed as he exclaimed, "That is not why people get out of your way, Mr. Hare, because we think you are important. Of course not," he said with a large dose of incredulity in his voice. "We get out of your way because you are going so fast that you almost bowl us over. What do you think you are missing when you race through the forest at such a high speed?" grunted Mr. Bowled-Over.

"Missing? Missing?" exclaimed the hare. "I am not missing anything. I am on my way to something very important when I am rushing. How could I be missing anything?"

"Do you notice the flowers? Do you notice the sunshine? Do you notice the people enjoying themselves in the park? Do you enjoy meeting the other animals around you and maybe spending some time chatting and catching up with their lives? Do you laugh with others? Do you ever even just take time for yourself?" Mr. Bowled-Over continued, firing questions in rapid succession. Then, almost as an afterthought, he added, "Do you even know where you are going?"

Mr. Hare was almost breathless at the very thought of so many questions in one ridiculously long sentence. "What are YOU in such a rush about?" he replied defensively, as if justifying his own behaviors by attacking Mr. Bowled-Over.

"Well, maybe I do miss some of these things when I rush around, but SO WHAT? I see them eventually, when I have stopped rushing. It is better than being like you, sitting around complaining about life and never going anywhere. You are always saying that you feel like life has bowled you over. Well that is not going to happen to me. No one is going to bowl me over!"

"Now, now," said Mr. Harrowed, finding himself in the unusual position of mediating between Mr. Hare and Mr. Bowled-Over (which he laughingly thought might feel like mediating between his worst self and his better self). "Maybe there is merit in both positions. Sometimes it is OK to rush (so long as you have a purpose) and sometimes it is OK to just sit and reflect on life (so long as you have a purpose)." Well, maybe that was the purpose. Anyway, he hoped he was convincing the two of them not to fight with each other, as he was feeling quite unnerved at the thought of his hosts being upset with each other.

"Moderation in all things," he heard himself say. Where did that come from? He thought. I have often heard my mother say that, but I never took her seriously.

"Moderation!" exclaimed Mr. Bowled Over. "Well, look who's talking! Perhaps instead of complaining about our names being too depressing for you, you should take a long look at your own. Mr. Harrowed, indeed. What do you think that says about you?"

Mr. Harrowed furrowed his brow and looked thoughtful and perplexed. He had never thought about that.

The State of Anxiety monthly refreshment meeting was ending. It was Mr. Counter-Dependent's job to close the meeting.

"Everyone feels that they have not enjoyed the meeting and that the refreshments, as always, have been disappointing. The meeting has been too long and none of us have appreciated having uninvited guests. Someone should have told us ahead of time that there were going to be strangers in our midst. Are there any closing comments before I declare this meeting adjourned?"

Mrs. People-Pleaser jumped to her feet.

"I would like to observe that despite our complaints, the tea, coffee, scones and cakes were devoured and the visitors have been subjected to just the kind of unwelcome behavior that one would expect from people who were constantly anxious. Just like every other meeting, if we did not like it, we would not keep doing it." She smiled at everyone and sat down.

"Oh really, Mrs. People Pleaser, you always paint much too rosy a picture of everything. Get real. Mr. Hare as always has done a poor job of leading the meeting. If I had been in charge things would have been much better."

Mr. Counter-Dependent thought he knew a thing or too about leadership, considering himself the ultimate example of how things should be and spending his life pushing back at people and judging others for not living up to his standards. Actually his middle name should have been "superiority." Ms. Co-dependent was looking very uncomfortable. She was trying to get Mr. Co-Dependent to be quiet, as she did not like it when he upset the others. She knew she needed them, even if he did not. Mr. Harrowed felt a tweaking in his stomach as he listened to Mr. Counter-Dependent's rhetoric. His somewhat arrogant attitude seemed all too familiar.

THE VILLAGE OF ILLUSIONS

Mrs. Saddled, Mr. Harrowed, the hare and the fawn bid the others farewell and headed off through the park together. Mrs. Saddled looked much more relaxed and stopped to enjoy the fragrance of the beautiful lilac trees on the avenue. Mr. Harrowed was also walking at a much slower pace and seemed to be taking in the energies of the moment rather than rushing on to the next. Everyone was enjoying just being together and time seemed irrelevant. It was as if the world were standing still.

"Oh, by the way, what would have happened if I had picked the left side of the park?" asked Mr. Harrowed, somewhat nonchalantly.

"The park shows you mirror images of your multiple selves. We all have many versions of ourselves, our sad self, our happy self, our co-dependent self, our harrowed self, etc. Choosing the other side would have led you to one of the other States you spend a lot of time in, but that is a story for another day," said the hare with a knowing look. Mr. Harrowed peered anxiously over his shoulder as if he were expecting some of his other selves to show up. He laughed as he thought about how much work it had been to begin to figure out his harrowed self. The thought of figuring out his other selves made him feel immediately tired.

Mr. Harrowed and Mrs. Saddled said goodbye to each other. "Perhaps you should call me Harry," said Mr. Harrowed, extending a gesture of friendship.

"Oh! Thanks, and perhaps you should call me Sara," said Mrs. Saddled, thinking to herself how much nicer it would be to use her first name from now on.

Sara wakened to the noise of the children, who had moved closer to her and were playing loudly just a few feet away. She started to shout over to them to be quiet, as she simultaneously put out her hand to make sure her package was still there. Then she remembered her dream. The shout never crossed her lips and she sat back on the bench to watch the children playing, trying to remember what it felt like to be a child herself.

As she walked away, she noticed Harry Harrowed wandering off in the distance. She waved knowingly to him as they parted company.

"Mrs., Mrs.!" a young voice yelled. "You have left your package."

"Ah, it is all right, young man," she said. "Actually, just call me Sara. It is OK; just leave the package there. Maybe someone else will need it. I am going to explore the rest of my life without it."

Sara began to walk away. "On second thoughts, why would I leave it for someone else? Let's get rid of it once and for all." She walked back towards the package, carefully picked it up and put it in a nearby trashcan. "There, now it's really gone."

The young boy shrugged his shoulders, looked puzzled for a moment, and went back to playing ball with his friends.

The State of People-Pleasing:

If you traveled just a little farther south from the State of Anxiety, you would have found the State of People-Pleasing and the scene there was very different. It was a beautiful day in the State of People-Pleasing. Everyone was dressed nicely and people were busying themselves with trying to find ways to please each other. A bad day in the State was when you went to bed believing that you had displeased someone. A very good day was when you knew you had pleased many people. The State of People-Pleasing was a predominantly female State. There were some men there, of course, and the women worked very hard to please them. What was not so obvious was that the men were also trying to please the women. Each of the women was wearing a different silk dress, but each dress was long and graceful. They looked very feminine and had golden threads flowing from the sleeves. The men were wearing well-designed silk shirts with an anchor logo on the pocket and olive green silk slacks with golden threads woven through the fabric. It was, on the surface, a happy and elegant place.

Eileen Affable was playing happily on the beach with her dog Sunny, when suddenly, as if from nowhere, a little boy appeared. He looked very pleased with himself and he said, "Hi, do you mind if I play with you? What a lovely dog."

"Of course you can play with me," said Eileen pleasantly, "but where did you come from and what is your name?"

"Oh, I came from Nowhere and my name is Minion."

"That's a strange name. It sounds very important, and how can you come from nowhere?"

"Actually, I am not very important at all," said Minion, "quite inconsequential really and I really do come from Nowhere."

"Oh, why do you say that?" cried Eileen. "We are all so happy here and no one is unimportant. Let's play for a while throwing a ball to Sunny. She'll run and catch it."

"OK," said Minion, and off they ran down the beach, with Sunny by their side looking very excited that she was finally getting attention.

They played together for quite a while and on one occasion Eileen threw the ball for Sunny and it rolled into the sand dunes.

Eileen and Minion ran in after the ball and as Eileen bent down to find it she discovered a hole in the ground that looked like it opened up to a

THE VILLAGE OF ILLUSIONS

cave leading beneath the ground. Minion looked quite disconcerted when he realized what she had found.

"Let's go and explore," cried Eileen. "This is very exciting."

"Actually," said Minion slowly, "that is the opening to where I live, you are welcome to come and visit, but are you sure you want to? It leads to Nowhere."

"Of course, silly, we are friends, aren't we? Let's go, it must lead somewhere," said Eileen.

Actually, it leads to Nowhere, thought Minion, but it was too late to stop Eileen.

The two friends and Sunny set off down the path that led from the cave door and soon came across a sign that directed them to Nowhere. As they followed the sign, Eileen began to notice many empty containers on the side of the road, some with people sitting next to them looking preoccupied, with vacant looks on their faces.

This feels a little spooky, thought Eileen. Maybe I should not have been so hasty in agreeing to visit here. Sunny was getting quite agitated and Eileen observed that she was staying close to her heels. She consoled herself with the fact that her new friend seemed quite at home and calm.

As they turned the next corner the road widened and right in front of them were large white gates. As they walked through the gates, they saw a horse and buggy coming towards them with a man driving it.

"Hello," called the man. "Welcome to Nowhere. Would you like a ride?"

They were very tired, as they had been running around the beach in the State of People-Pleasing all day, just trying to please each other (and themselves, of course).

"Oh yes, please," called Minion as they all jumped aboard.

Eileen noticed that it was not quite dark, but it was not light either. She asked Minion what time it was and he said he did not know. He told her that it was always dusk in their State.

Eileen thought that perhaps it was time to go home. She was getting anxious and she was hungry. Minion, as if reading her mind, said, "You must be starving. Let's go inside and have some food."

Go inside where? She thought, just as a very grand building appeared in front of them. Town Hall, City of Nowhere, The State of Insignificance, the sign read.

The State of Insignificance! That did not sound nearly as much fun as the State of People-Pleasing, she thought to herself. She dared not share that thought with Minion.

Eileen ordered a mug of hot chocolate and a peppermint stick, and then plucked up her courage to ask Minion, "Where is the State of Insignificance and why do people live here? Why do you live here?"

Minion, who had not felt he was entitled to something as grand as hot chocolate, was sipping on a glass of cold milk, looked skeptically at her and said, "Well, if you must know, it is situated directly underneath the State of People-Pleasing and people here feel as if they are not important. They used to try very hard to please people and then they just got tired; they ran out of energy, so they decided to live down here instead. It is sort of an apathetic State, no one has very much energy and everyone just sits around and wonders why he or she should bother. You see, even in the State of People-Pleasing people are worrying about not being noticed and that is why they try so hard. People down here have come to terms with the belief that no one notices them, they are not important and they are not missed. We believe the glass is always half empty, if not entirely empty and the people you saw at the edge of the road with empty containers have been here the longest and are waiting to go to the State of Resentment. I have heard talk that the State of Resentment is directly beneath us, but I have not been there." He hesitated and then added, "I am told though, that if you stay here long enough you eventually end up in the State of Resentment."

Oh dear, thought Eileen, that is a very troublesome story. "But why are you here? Why are the children here? Are you not too young to be feeling apa........ what did you call it ....apathic?"

"No, silly, apathetic. Well, you are right, maybe I am too young, but the trouble is that the adults who live here have children and the children watch how the adults live and they copy them. Some of us try to get out as we suspect there is a world outside of our feelings of insignificance. I was exploring a different way to use my energy when I visited you today on the beach, but here I am, back where I belong, I guess. I am really worried that if I stay here long enough they will make me move to the State of Resentment, which as I explained, I have heard is an awful place to live."

Eileen thought about this for a long while as she continued to drink her hot chocolate. "What about the State of People-Pleasing? We are happy there; at least I think we are. Nevertheless, you are saying that when people get tired, they come here. Does that mean we are not really happy? And are the children copying the adults also?" she asked hurriedly.

Their driver was sitting off in a corner drinking his tea and minding his own business. Looking quite disinterested and yet at the same time drawn to join in the conversation, he said, "Well, young lady, I suppose people are happy there. It is just that they might be being happy for the wrong reasons. Trying so hard to please is too much work and I think your heart gets very tired and you kind of set yourself up for rejection. It is good to please others, but you also have to please yourself.

"You are still young," he explained. "Why don't you take a look at a different path for yourself? You have more freedom to choose than you realize. So do you, young Minion."

Eileen had never thought about living anywhere else, but thinking about that possibility, she began to speculate about a different future. Perhaps she should follow her passion, explore her dreams instead of living a reality that other people wanted for her. She started to daydream about a life full of potential and possibilities; a life where she could define her own happiness and not be dependent on pleasing others.

Eileen suddenly found herself and Sunny back on the beach. As she was walking back towards her home and thinking that perhaps she should ask her mother if she could go away to college after all, she saw someone waving to her in the distance. As she squinted through the sun, she realized it was Minion running towards her. Oh, how wonderful, she thought, Minion has decided to make a stand for his own freedom also.

Amethyst looked over at Patience, who was gazing intently in the direction of Eileen and Minion.

"What are you thinking?" she asked. "You look like you are miles away."

Startled from her thoughts, Patience answered, "I was miles away. I was thinking about my life and wondering how much time I have spent in negative states instead of following my passions? I can relate to so many of the negative states. I have spent hours, maybe even days living in some of them. I suspect even the State of Resentment has had my undivided attention on occasions." Finding her thoughts a bit overwhelming, Patience began to rationalize them. "Perhaps it is just part of the human condition? Maybe people experience all of these States, even if they are fundamentally happy people. What do you think, Amethyst?"

"I think that there may be a grain of truth in that. If someone gets stuck living in a state of anxiety then that becomes a negative coping pattern, a way of being, and of course creates problems for them. The challenge is to be able to see yourself, catch the patterns of behavior you have created and to ask yourself how that pattern continues to serve you. What are the advantages of continuing to behave like that?" offered Amethyst.

"What do you mean by that? I don't see any advantages to being in a negative state," exclaimed Patience.

"Well, let me see if I can give you an example. Imagine that you are a happy child and you notice that you get more attention from your mother when you are sad than you do when you are happy. You may unconsciously develop the habit of being sad in order to get your mother's attention. The problem with that is that while it may have worked with your mother, it does not serve you well in the end. It deprives you of your own happiness and probably drives other people away. Sometimes people remain unhappy, acting like victims, for example, in order to control the attention of others, or because they think it keeps them safe."

Patience thought about that for a while and then grimaced. "I am going to have to keep thinking about that," she said.

On the path:

The humming bird flew swiftly across the pond and deftly caught the end of the wind chimes, ringing them gently in the breeze. Amethyst and Patience looked around and noticed Mrs. Baker at the bottom of the driveway. Amethyst was pleased. Mrs. Baker had listened to Woody and was beginning her own personal growth journey.

Amethyst moved towards one of the oak trees and picked up a handful of the gold dust that was lying on the ground around the base of the anchor. She threw it in the general direction of Mrs. Baker and much to Patience's amazement, she found herself listening in to Mrs. Baker's innermost thoughts, like walking around inside her mind.

Mrs. Baker was daydreaming as she strolled along Inner Wisdom Avenue.

Wow, this is a very tranquil place, the oak trees are strikingly majestic and I love the pond and the animals, especially the turtles. This is a peaceful place where I can relax and allow myself some reflection time. I have been feeling so anxious recently. I have been longing to go and sit on top of a mountain and just daydream, or even just sit on the beach and watch the tide come in and out. This place seems to fit the bill. All of the mini-dramas I have been involved in recently. I feel so anxious and almost indignant that these things have been happening to me. I am a nice person, how can so many things be going wrong? I am weary of the stories that rumble around in my head about how other people had treated me. There are so many people I find threatening and that is exhausting. Somehow, I suspect all of these mini-dramas are related and perhaps even of my own making. But? It's not that other people are entirely innocent.

Alice Baker stopped to pick up a piece of oyster shell from the path she was walking along. As she examined the shell and thought how delicate it was, her thoughts continued.

I seem to be the common denominator in all of the stories. There is a pattern here and I am not sure that I like what I am seeing. I seem to spend a lot of time trying to please people, feeling under-appreciated and often rejected, resenting it and then feeling victimized. Perhaps my self-esteem is not very strong. When I was working in the kitchen the other evening, my inner voice was telling me not to blame other people. What would the ramifications be of not blaming others and instead seeing myself as the central character, and the driving force in this drama I call my life? Bob has always said that I had a choice about what attitude I adopted. Perhaps he is right. If only I could work out how to think more positively and change the tone of the stories that rattle around in my head.

As soon as she had that thought, it seemed like many threads started to unravel in front of her and questions were flashing across her mind.

What are the reasons I get so emotionally attached to situations? What would happen if I were more low-key? What if I stopped being such a drama queen and became more calm, more circumspect, less self-absorbed? Would life be boring? Would I be more joyful? What would happen? Why do I feel so compelled to be a people-pleaser, to defend people? Why do I care so much about what they think of me? I wonder if I could see myself from other people's perspective. Do they see me as sometimes needy? Too much people-pleasing? Too outspoken? I think my friends still love me, despite my worst self, but why do I try so hard to prove myself to people? Would they still love me and want me if I became less extroverted? Less needy? I am afraid I might become too distant and then no one would want to know me.

Connecting the Dots:

Amethyst had been watching Mrs. Baker, listening intently to her inner dialog, and was impressed with her progress. She decided she would give her a little assistance, perhaps some additional insights. She indicated for Patience to follow her very quietly.

Amethyst motioned with her right hand and two bluebirds flew over to a glass shelf that contained another silver needle. They gently picked the needle up and flew back over to her, placing it carefully on her lap. Amethyst looked through the inner eye of the needle. What she saw was very interesting and enlightening and she hoped that Alice Baker would benefit from the wisdom of seeing her childhood from a different perspective.

Mrs. Baker was deep in her own thoughts and oblivious to Amethyst and Patience as she walked down the road. There were a series of golden threads all tangled up and lying on the ground. Mrs. Baker did not appear to notice them, but Amethyst picked up one of the threads and began to follow it. As it unraveled, she came across a little girl crying as she sat on a wall at the edge of the village. Amethyst stopped to inquire if she could help.

"My mother is angry at me. I was baking peanut butter cookies and I spilled all of the flour on the floor. She yelled at me. She said I was clumsy and stupid and did not know how to do anything properly," the little girl sobbed through her tears.

"I ran out of the kitchen and came here," said young Alice, swinging her legs off the edge of the village wall as she wiped her tears.

"Why are you sitting here?" asked Amethyst.

"This is where I always come when I am in trouble. It's right at the edge of the village."

"Is it one of your favorite places?" Amethyst asked.

"Well, I come here a lot. I like the sunflowers," she said as she pointed at the array of sunflowers on the ground beneath her feet. "I like the way they turn their faces towards the sun."

"Oh, then it makes you happy when you come here?"

"Not really, but I like the sunflowers. When I am happy I stay home and play with my little brother and talk to my daddy. I come here when I am sad and when my mother is angry with me. I come here and wonder if they would care if I ran away. Then I watch the sunflowers and wonder why my mom cannot always be sunny and cheerful. She is always saying mean things. I don't think she likes me."

"It is difficult to please your mother then?" asked Amethyst.

Alice nodded slowly.

"Are there any times when your mother is happy with you?"

"When I am taking care of my little brother," she added. "I always have to look out for him. That is the only way to please my mother."

Just then, Alice saw her brother coming down the road and ran off to join him.

Amethyst reached for another golden thread and began to follow it. This time she and Patience found themselves in the middle of a large room where it seemed people were getting ready for a birthday party.

"Alice! Can you run to the corner store and pick up the candles for your brother's birthday cake?" yelled a woman from the far side of the room.

Alice was nowhere in sight.

THE VILLAGE OF ILLUSIONS

"Alice, where are you?" The woman yelled.

Alice came running into the room. "What do you need, Mother?"

Her mother repeated the request and Alice willingly ran off to the corner store, returning shortly with the candles.

Her brother was playing in the yard with his friends when she arrived back. "I got the candles for your birthday cake," she declared proudly. "I know you like candles. I know you like birthday cake. You're going to enjoy your party, aren't you?" Alice said, not stopping for breath between each sentence.

Her brother continued playing, barely thanking her for her efforts and Alice, feeling under appreciated, went inside to find out what else her mother needed.

Patience began to feel sad. She could see that Alice was trying so hard to please and yet she could see that the people in her life did not seem to notice or appreciate her efforts and Alice was feeling rejected. Patience felt that she could identify with this as she also had spent many years doing the same thing -- helping others and not feeling valued. What was the answer?

As Amethyst was watching this scene unfold, another thread fell on the floor in front of her. She indicated to Patience to pick it up. This time they found themselves in a restaurant where Alice and her brother were having lunch together. Alice was older now and had left home to attend college. As Amethyst and Patience approached the table, they realized that Alice and her brother were having an argument.

"You can't trust her," said Alice. "She will always let you down. You know that is just the way she is. She is controlling, demanding and unreasonable and she says the meanest things. I cannot stand it when she says she loves us because her behavior never matches her words. Huh! What is love anyway?"

"Yes, Alice, I understand how you feel. I know that is the way she is, but after all, she is our mother."

"Don't you realize that if you tell her what you want to do that she will find fault and be nasty, just like she has done to me. I am telling you, you had better be careful. She is always talking negatively about us."

"I'm sure you are right, Alice, but I can't let being afraid of Mother control my life, and anyway, I am a man and she will not interfere with my life as much as she has interfered with yours."

"Well, don't tell me I didn't warn you," said Alice.

"Oh dear," whispered Patience. "I am afraid Alice is learning that she cannot trust people, that they will hurt her if she lets her guard down."

"Does any of that sound familiar, Patience?" asked Amethyst.

"Wow, Amethyst, you sure don't let a person off the hook do you?" laughed Patience.

"This is your dream, Patience. You are in charge of what you want to see this evening," responded Amethyst with a good-humored grin.

"OK! OK! You are right, some of it does sound vaguely familiar. Nevertheless, in my case it is not all about my mother, at least I do not think it is. My mother is not quite as mean as Alice's mother, although she does not trust people and I have learned not to trust people. I keep my guard up and I am very counter-dependent to authority," said Patience with a sigh of resignation.

"You sound quite defensive, Patience. It is not my intention to make you feel defensive. This is your work to do, at your pace. So if you are not ready to deal with the issue, that is entirely up to you. Perhaps it will take more time, more dreams and more awareness before you can unravel some of this."

Patience felt bad. She had not intended to react defensively and the last thing she really wanted was to upset Amethyst.

"I am sorry, Amethyst. Please forgive me; it's just that all of this has come as quite a shock. When the story began, I thought I was watching someone else's movie and the more I watch the more I realize that this is my movie. It is quite sobering to realize that what we dislike in others is most probably a piece of ourselves," said Patience.

Amethyst reached over and put her arm on Patience's shoulder and said, "It is also true that what we like in others is a piece of ourselves."

"You know, Patience, some people never even ask the questions you have asked tonight, so although it doesn't feel like it, you are making progress. Socrates said that the unexamined life was not worth living and at least you are examining your life," offered Amethyst by way of consolation for Patience's obvious discomfort.

Amethyst wrapped up the threads from Mrs. Baker's story and handed them to the two blue jays with instructions to take them to the appropriate library on Inner Wisdom Avenue.

Alice Baker, in the meantime, had found herself thinking about her childhood. Perhaps it made sense to her now. She was beginning to see the connections. Her need to please, her fear of rejection, her need to warn her friends about people who might hurt them, were all being driven by her relationships with her past, and particularly her feelings about her mother. It was all there, just like pieces of a jigsaw puzzle. Why did she not see it sooner? She was convinced there was more to it than just her relationship with her mother. However, that would have to wait for another day. Regardless of the causes, now that she realized some of what was driving her, perhaps she should work on letting go and not holding on so tightly. She would learn to flow with life and not struggle against it.

As Alice Baker approached the Crystal Palace at the top of the driveway, a butterfly fluttered past her. Two blue jays away in the distance seemed to be carrying the remnants of what looked like golden threads and were tying them around an oak tree. That is so cute, she thought, smiling at them as she passed. Just at that moment, the bells in the clock tower chimed, making Amethyst smile.

Postscript:

Today it was Senior Turtle's turn to read. The animals and the fish were very excited. Octogenarian had told them ahead of time that Senior Turtle had a new angle on Mrs. Baker's story. They could not wait to hear it. Senior Turtle explained that they were going to share a story about Alice Baker's mother.

Annie Whistlestop was feeling very anxious. She was the mother of two young children, a son and a daughter. She had to work very hard every day to take care of her children. Her husband was a decent man who worked long hours at the coalmines, a dirty and dangerous job. He came home late every night, but Annie did not mind because she was just glad he was safe for another day. Most days he was too tired to spend any quality time with his children, it was all he could do to eat dinner and then fall asleep.

Annie had visited one of her close friends earlier that day.

"I don't feel like a very good mother. You know I adopted these two kids and I am very proud of both of them. But I worry about Alice. She needs to become tougher if she is going to survive in the world. She seems very innocent," Annie told her friend.

"I am not worried about my son, as boys are usually OK."

She confided in her friend that she thought maybe she was a little hard on Alice, but she said, "I feel I have to toughen her up. I make many demands on her, but it is because I love her and I want her to have the skills to cope with anything that comes her way. Trouble is," she mused aloud, "once you start being so strict it is difficult to break the habit. My mother was tough on me. All I know is that I love my children and I have done my very best. Alice is very bright and very strong willed and frankly, I find her quite a handful. There are days when I think, despite her being a child, she is stronger than I am and I do not know how to cope with her. I hope she will be OK."

Senior Turtle continued....

Mrs. Baker's mother had been doing her best in the only way she knew. The fact that it was not enough, the fact that it damaged Alice Baker, had never been her intention. As Alice Baker was now realizing, not only were there layers and layers of pain, there were also layers and layers of complexities hidden in her past. A past to which, it seemed, she was still reacting. A past that was replete with people doing their best, no matter how inadequate. Forgiving people who are doing their best and most probably meant you no harm is not always easy. That is part of our ongoing work. The ghosts and spirits of childhood haunt and inspire us throughout our lives. (Bentz 1989)

Patience was wide eyed as she sat listening to Senior Turtle.

"I cannot believe how many similarities there are between Alice Baker and me. I feel as if I know her and her whole family," said Patience.

"You have had quite an evening, Patience, and I hope that I have managed to help you see that the answers to some of your questions about inner wisdom have been living inside of you all the time. You only have to tap into them. I have two more stories I would like you to experience, and this time I am going to select them for you," said Amethyst, beckoning as she did for Patience to follow her to the biggest oak tree in the avenue.

Chapter Eight
The Happiness Bug

*Whenever I stand on the leading edge of my own learning
I am confident that I will land on either solid ground, or I
will be taught to fly.
(Turnbull 2003) adapted from anonymous quote*

On a Mission:

Woody was in a terrible rush that day. He flew into Flapper's house flapping his wings and saying, "Flapper, I need your help. We have to go on a trip. Amethyst has given us a very important project. Call Mr. & Mrs. Blue Jay and ask them if they will come with us also. We need all the help we can get." Woody had lived in the State of Inner Wisdom for as long as he could remember. Amethyst frequently sent him on important errands to visit people in the State of Reality, but today's assignment was the biggest ever.

"What is it, Woody?" asked Flapper, catching the excitement and realizing that he was being recruited for a very important project.

"Amethyst thinks they have lost the Happiness Bug and she has asked us to go and look for it," blurted Woody. "She says she has witnessed an epidemic of people who are arriving at the State of Inner Wisdom feeling lost and unhappy. She is most concerned that something insidious is happening to the people in State of Reality. It seems they have lost the ability to be happy and she thinks something may have happened to the Happiness Bug."

Flapper was aghast at this information. He lived quite a secure life really, safe in the knowledge that the world around him was peaceful and predictable. The very idea that happiness was missing filled him with horror. Of course, he must rise to the occasion and accompany Woody on his quest. He would call Mr. & Mrs. Blue Jay immediately, but first, which comes before immediately, he had some questions for Woody.

"What else did Amethyst tell you? Did she give us any clues about what it looks like, or where we might begin to look for it?"

"All I know is that Amethyst is worried. She said she is concerned that too many people seem to be unhappy these days. So, she has asked us to go and investigate," said Woody.

The four friends set off later that afternoon, deciding after some deliberations, to fly north. After a few hours, they stopped for a rest. They flew onto an overhead cable overlooking a village green. Beneath them people were scurrying around, all looking very busy and clearly rushing off to somewhere.

"I wonder where we are?" asked Flapper.

"Not sure," said Woody, "but let's try to find out," he said as he flew over to a sign that was outside a large building.

"Productivity City Hall," read the sign.

"Oh, we must be in the City of Productivity, which is in the State of Worthiness," said Woody knowingly.

They flew around for a while and eventually they came to a building where there was lots of activity. There was a perpetual stream of traffic in and out of the building. The four birds landed on a branch of a nearby tree. As people were entering and leaving, they were dropping a package into a large container at the door.

Flapper was curious. "What is that about, Cousin Woody?"

"I am not sure. Let's fly closer for a better look," said Woody.

Woody landed on the edge of the container and looked inside. "It is full of bags," he said in amazement.

Flapper, who was gliding towards the container from the other side, said, "The sign says 'leave your baggage at the door.'"

Mr. Blue Jay was flapping around in an excitable manner.

"Wow!" he said. "They drop their baggage in this container whether they are coming or going, ensuring that they don't take it inside and also that they don't take any baggage they get inside on to their next encounter. Now, that is interesting. We need to take that idea to the people in the State of Reality, as they are always carrying around lots of baggage. Do you remember Mrs. Saddled? Poor Mrs. Saddled, she carried that package around for years. It got heavier and heavier but she never seemed to realize she had the option to put it down until the day she was lucky enough to get invited to the Refreshment break meeting."

"Oh yes, dear," said Mrs. Blue Jay, "and do you also remember Mr. Harrowed who rushed around so much he had no time to stop and drop his baggage at the door? He just kept landing it on everyone he bumped into," she added.

"Well the people here look happy enough, so it must be working," observed Flapper. Woody and the others laughed.

Flapper looked puzzled. "What are you laughing at?" he asked, feigning hurt indignation.

"We were not sure if you meant that the people were happy because they were working, or the people were happy because they could drop their baggage at the door," explained Woody in a brotherly tone.

"Oh! I see. Well, I think I do," said Flapper.

"Do you think work makes people feel better?" asked Mrs. Blue jay curiously.

"I think being productive and having a sense of accomplishment makes people feel better, yes," said Woody.

"I can understand that," said Mrs. Blue Jay. "I always feel much better when I am busy."

"Huh! Is that all it takes to make people happy then, just keep them busy?" asked Flapper. "Is that what it takes to find the happiness bug? Just work hard and feel productive?"

"I don't think it is that simple," said Woody. "Let's keep exploring and maybe we can find out." With that he spread his wings and took off.

The four friends flew overnight and in the early morning they arrived at a river. It was a river so large it almost looked like the ocean. They could smell the fresh morning air and as they flew down to the water's edge, they saw a very large white bird sitting on a rock.

CAPTAIN FORAGER

"Hello, my name is Flapper, what is yours?" called Flapper, who was always the most outgoing and friendly of the group.

"Well, hello to you," replied the seagull. "My name is Captain Forager, welcome to my territory. You must have traveled far. I don't usually see the likes of you so close to the sea."

Flapper was not sure how to take that remark. As he preferred to be polite, he decided to ignore it and give Captain Forager the benefit of the doubt. I wonder what he is Captain of, anyway, Flapper pondered quietly to himself.

"So, what brings you here?" continued Captain Forager in a mildly more pleasant tone.

"We are touring, sort of like a holiday, doing some research along the way, and we saw the river and thought it looked like a nice place to stop and have a rest," said Mrs. Blue Jay, not wanting to disclose their mission and at the same time anxious to make sure they did not offend their new host. After all, he looked a lot bigger and more imposing than any of them.

"Oh, well then, you have come to the right place if you are looking for a holiday. This is a favorite vacation spot," said Captain Forager.

"Where can we find the people?" said Mr. Blue Jay, getting himself ready for another day's adventure.

"It is early, but if you just wait here with me, they will be along shortly. This is their favorite spot on the beach. Meantime, enjoy the view and have some breakfast."

It was indeed a lovely view filled with tranquility and splendor. The river was wide and expansive and off to the left there were green rolling hills, shrouded in an early morning mist. This particular part of the river was very wide and was more like an estuary leading from the ocean to the narrower part of the river and the main shipping ports. Across the river in the distance, they could see a white lighthouse and the early morning ferries sailing past. What a beautiful sight! When you looked to the right, you could see in the distance a very majestic and imposing pier stretching out into the water, obviously waiting for some of those ferries to come and visit.

Along the beach, there were large grey slate rocks that were perfect for climbing on, or, if you were a bird, for perching on. Nestled in between the rocks was a myriad of little water pools full of crabs and other interesting creatures of the sea. The rocks closer to the water were home to seaweed and mussels, which the tide had left behind. The beach itself was very rocky with precious little sand in sight. At the top of the beach, there were about a dozen rowing boats all cleaned and ready for the day and

THE VILLAGE OF ILLUSIONS

behind them was a series of colorful huts which housed canvas striped deck chairs and a small coffee shop. As Woody and his friends sat on the rocks taking in the depth and breadth of the beautiful scenery, they could smell the seaweed in the fresh salt air, hear the seagulls talking to each other and watch the early morning sun burn off the mist from the hills, getting itself ready for another perfect day. Flapper thought that perhaps they had already found the happiness bug; just looking at this view was enough to make him happy, at least.

"Let's fly over and check out that pier," said Flapper, always anxious to extend his adventure.

"OK," said the others, "let's go."

En route to the pier, they saw a very picturesque main street lined with attractive stone cottages with lots of flowers and flowering hedges in the front gardens. There was a row of shops serving this community; a dairy where people were picking up their morning allowance of cream and milk; a bakery where they were serving fresh baked morning rolls; the butcher's, where people would come for their fresh dinner meats; and the newsagent ready to sell the news of the day. The pharmacy and the hardware stores were not open yet, as they knew that people did not need them until later in the day. There were a few people walking around, but you could tell that this small town was not yet awake.

Opposite the pier was a very stately old hotel, painted in white with black trim. The hotel had turrets and a large front patio, with an imposing staircase leading to the front entrance. It looked like a warm and special place and was probably a source of comfort and enjoyment for the people who stayed there. At the pier, there was another newsagent, obviously there for the commuters as they rushed to catch their ferries to the mainland. The four friends flew onto the pier and landed on one of the metal bollards that held the ropes from the ships as they docked.

"You know," said Mrs. Blue Jay, sounding as if she were about to make a very profound announcement, "it seems strange to me that a small town which looks so idyllic and picturesque, and where people come on holiday to get away from it all, has two newsagents. Wouldn't you think that people would want to get away from the news when they were on holiday?"

Mr. Blue Jay cocked his beak to one side and looked at his wife, thinking, not for the first time, about how bright she was. "You are right, my dear. What an interesting observation."

"After all," said Mrs. Blue Jay, pleased to have her husband's validation of her observation, "they don't have two bakeries or two dairies or even two butcher shops."

There was not much else to do with that conversation other than to acknowledge the wisdom of it, so the four friends redirected their attention to the imminent arrival of a very large ferry. The ferry was black with a large yellow stripe along the length of the vessel and a yellow funnel with a black stripe sat proudly on top of the pilot's cabin. Following the ship, flying directly above the picturesque white waters churning from the ship's propellers, were a multitude of seagulls. They were all squawking together in a melodic tone, which added to the ambience.

"It is one of life's mysteries," said Woody, catching the philosophical drift that Mrs. Blue Jay had started.

"What is?" asked Flapper, thinking he was being left behind.

"The fact that seagulls follow ships. It is not as if people are throwing food off the stern. They do not look as if they are fishing and they are certainly not lost. So why do they do it?"

The four friends flew up on to the roof of the pier building, having thought it sensible to vacate the metal bollard before the ship came gently alongside. They were still thinking about the seagulls as they watched the ship dock and the deck hands rush forward with the gangplanks to let the people disembark.

Eventually Mr. Blue Jay said, "Maybe there is no reason. Perhaps they just do it because they enjoy it."

"Possibly," said Woody. "It could be possible that they like the feel of the wind and the cooling mist from the water in their face and they are just doing it for fun."

"They are certainly not reading the newspaper," laughed Mrs. Blue Jay. They all laughed at the thought and decided to fly back to the beach.

On the way, they spotted a little girl and boy coming down a lane at the side of one of the cottages. They were laughing and talking as they walked. When they reached the main road, they stopped and looked both ways to make sure that there was no traffic coming and then they ran across the road towards the beach.

"Shall we walk on the road or go along the rocks this morning?" asked the girl.

"Are you daft? Of course we will go along the rocks, it is the only way to go," said the boy. "Come on, I'll race you to the railings."

They both laughed and set off at a fast pace towards the metal railings, which led to their favorite part of the beach. When they reached the railings they had to stop and catch their breath, but more importantly they always had a little gymnastic routine they did at the railings. The middle bar on the railing was missing, allowing someone of his or her size and flexibility to use the top railing as a gymnastic bar. They always competed for who could do the best gyrations around that bar before they were ready to climb down to the rocks below. They played with joyful innocence for about ten minutes before deciding to move on. They knew they needed to return in time for breakfast, but for the moment time was standing still, responsibility, and accountability had faded into the background.

As they ran along the rocks, they were both extremely sure-footed and the birds flying above thought to themselves that the children had played on these rocks many times before. The little girl headed for a piece of rock that she told her brother was her favorite rock because it looked as if a set of stairs had been carved into the side of it. Sure enough, there were three little steps on the face of the rock, not big enough for her entire foot, but big enough that if you only put your toes on them you could carefully climb to the top of the rock. She always enjoyed doing that. Her brother, on the other hand, delighted in ferreting around in the rock pools, looking for crabs. The bigger the crab, the more delighted he was.

After a while he shouted over to her, "Come on, let's play skimmers."

"OK, I'm coming," she called. They both ran to the water's edge and found as many small flat rocks as they could. They were actually small sections of the grey slate that had broken away and been worn down by the ocean. They proceeded to throw them on the water, counting the number of times they skimmed the surface before they sank.

"I got six that time. See if you can beat that," shouted her brother.

Always one to rise to the challenge, the little girl picked up the flattest rock she could find, slowly pulled her arm back and let the rock fly. It bounced on the surface eight times and she jumped up and down with delight. Her brother laughed and started looking for a bigger rock.

Being the older sister and suddenly overcome by feelings of responsibility, she called, "Come on, I'm hungry. Let's go back for breakfast."

"OK, but later I am going to find a skimmer that will do twelve!" he informed her gallantly.

Woody commented on how spontaneous and free the children seemed as the four friends watched them run back along the rocks, presumably to eat a well-deserved breakfast. Speaking of breakfast, it was time to take Captain Forager up on his suggestion.

Later that day the children returned, this time with an entourage of parents, two younger sisters, their uncles, aunts, cousins and grandparents. In deference to the adults, who were most definitely less limber, they walked along the road and not on the rocks. When they reached the beach the adults rented deck chairs, picked their favorite spot on the beach, got into their swimsuits and promptly sat down to enjoy the sun. The children ran on to the beach to play, urging their uncle and father to take them out on a rowing boat.

"Go for a swim for now and we will go out on a boat later," promised their fathers, hoping for at least an hour of relaxation before they had to go out and row a boat.

"So, this is what relaxation looks like," said Flapper, observing all of the activities. "They are just like the seagulls that follow the ships."

"What do you mean?" said Mr. Blue Jay.

"Well, they are doing things just because they like it. I mean, what is the purpose of lying around in the sun on a piece of canvas held up by some wood? They must be doing it for fun. They are leaping in and out of the water, splashing each other as they go. What is the point in that?"

"I don't know. Do you think we have found a clue to the Happiness Bug?" asked Flapper.

"I am not sure, Mr. Blue Jay. This is the State of Recreation and Relaxation, and yet, I cannot help but feel there is more to it," said Woody. "They seem to be laughing a lot, which is good. Surely, happiness is not just reserved for when they go on holiday. Don't you think they could learn to do that back at the State of Reality also?"

"Maybe it would help if they took things less seriously over there," said Mrs. Blue Jay in a reflective tone. "I saw a sign somewhere, a long time ago that said, *'If you can solve your problems, then what is the need of worrying and if you cannot solve them, then what is the use of worrying.'*" (Thondup 1998).

"You are right, but they come here to get away from it all. Sadly though, Captain Forager tells me that this vacation spot is not as busy as it used to be because people are working harder and harder and taking less and less time to relax and enjoy themselves."

"Yes, but think of all the hours they live in the State of Reality and the few short hours of their lives they live in the State of Relaxation," said Mr. Blue Jay.

"So, is that what it takes to make people happy? A little work, a sense of accomplishment, a place to deposit your baggage, and a sprinkling of recreation and relaxation?" asked Flapper.

"I am not sure," said Woody, "but perhaps we are getting closer."

The four friends watched everyone having fun and when the children finally persuaded their fathers to take them out in the rowing boats, they decided it was time to move on. They bade farewell to Captain Forager and then followed the small rowing boats as they headed west towards the rolling hills, eventually taking their leave of them, flying further west

THE VILLAGE OF ILLUSIONS

towards the State of Esteem and still in search of the elusive Happiness Bug.

"What does it look like?" asked Flapper.

"What does WHAT look like?" said Woody.

"The Happiness Bug, of course!"

"Good question, Flapper. I'm not sure. Amethyst says that some people seem never to be without it and others spend their life chasing it. Some never let it in and still others have it and then lose it," answered Woody, trying to sound as helpful as he could while knowing he was not really answering the question.

"Well, that is very interesting and intriguing but not very helpful. We still don't know what it looks like, so how are we going to know when we find it?" said Flapper in an exasperated tone.

Mrs. Blue Jay caught the drift of the intrigue and added, "Is it really a bug? Does it look like a bug? Like a caterpillar, for example? Alternatively, maybe it is like a disease. You know, people talk about catching the flu bug. Maybe that's it. Maybe it's infectious?"

"I don't know," said Woody, "but let's keep trying to find out. I have a feeling that it is a bit like piecing together a jigsaw puzzle. We have to keep looking for the pieces that fit together."

The four friends flew on and finally arrived in the State of Esteem where they found themselves drawn towards the roof of a building, which looked like the one they had found in the State of Productivity. Sure enough, people were rushing in and out of this building, too. If they did not know any better, they would have thought it was a colony of ants. They noticed a small building at the end of the complex and flew over to investigate. The sign on the door said "S. Steem Sports Facility." The four friends looked at each other in amazement. What was this about? They flew along the side of the building, which was mainly glass. What they saw were pieces of exercise equipment labeled Steem Stair Climber, Steem Treadmill and Steem Weight Lifting. There was another room in the corner named the Steem Room. Curiosity was getting the better of them. What did this mean? They flew back to the front of the building to hover in the hopes of overhearing some conversations and did not have to wait long. Two women were walking towards the front door.

"Wow! What a day. My boss was in a foul mood today and made me feel that everything I did for him was wrong. Just dropping my baggage at the door is not enough to help me get my head straight after that onslaught of negativity. I really need some Steem Therapy tonight."

"Huh! You think you had a bad day. You should try working for the woman who is my boss. She has to be the most demanding person I have ever met. I feel perpetually stressed out whenever she is around. She emanates such negative energy that you can feel her coming five minutes before she arrives," said the second woman. "Bring on the Steem Room, I say."

"You know, I come in to work in the morning feeling good about myself, and I would say that I have pretty strong self esteem, but a few hours working for her and I feel as if my positive self esteem is a puddle on the floor. She completely drains my energy. Thank goodness I can come here for an hour, recharge my batteries and rebuild my self image."

"Hah! I knew it! It is not as simple as dropping your baggage at the door," said Mrs. Blue Jay. "There is more to it than that."

"Oh, most definitely!" said Woody, trying to sound worldly. "It sounds as if when people feel badly treated at work and they need to de-stress themselves and rebuild their self esteem they come to the S. Steem Sports Facility."

"Is working out at the sports facility part of being happy?" asked Mrs. Blue Jay.

"I don't think so," said Woody wisely. "It feels to me as if they are actually using the facility as a coping mechanism to keep them healthy and to stop them from becoming dysfunctional."

"Oh, you mean it is the same as when we say, 'Calm down or you will pop a feather,'" said Flapper. Woody and the others laughed at the comparison.

"Well, yes, it is probably a bit like that, Flapper."

The four friends decided it was time to move on and to find a place to rest overnight. They flew for quite a few miles and as the sun was setting they found a nice tree to rest on.

As they were settling down for the evening, Mrs. Blue Jay said, "Do you think we are any closer to finding the happiness bug, Woody?"

"Oh! Mrs. Blue Jay," yawned Woody, "I wish I knew. Let us recap what we think we know so far. Why don't we each try to remember something we have learned?"

"I think being productive is part of it," said Flapper.

"Yes, and being able to deposit your baggage at the door," added Mr. Blue Jay.

"Oh! And, of course, being able to go on vacation and have lots of fun, rest and relaxation," added Mrs. Blue Jay.

"And also having positive self esteem," added Flapper.

"Well, that is a good list," said Woody, "but there is just one problem with it!" Everyone was tired and not looking for problems at that time of night, but they all turned towards Woody and said, "What?"

THE VILLAGE OF ILLUSIONS

"Well," said Woody, "I think it's possible to be productive and not happy and I think it is possible to be on vacation and not be happy and if you have to deposit your baggage, doesn't that mean you are still carrying it around? And, I bet it is possible to have positive self esteem and be quite obnoxious."

The others groaned. "Oh! Woody, how insightful of you," said Flapper. "In all probability you are correct. Therefore, we most likely have to keep looking. Goodnight everyone, get some rest. It looks like we have another long day ahead of us."

The next morning Woody and Flapper awakened to the sounds of Mr. and Mrs. Blue Jay chirping together and flying around the tree looking for breakfast. "Gosh, you two are early risers," said Flapper. "I am not really an early morning bird. I like to quietly walk around under the bushes and wake up slowly."

"Come on, let's go," cried Woody. "We have a busy day ahead of us."

The four birds flew east for most of the morning, heading in the direction of the State of Addictions. When they arrived, they saw a large parkland area where there was a lot of activity. They flew down to investigate. They settled on the branches of a very large oak tree and watched the activities below. There were many adults enjoying themselves, laughing, joking, and playing games.

"They certainly look like they are having a very good time together," said Flapper. "Yes, they do," said Woody. "I wonder what they are celebrating?"

Mrs. Blue Jay flew down for a closer look. When she returned to the tree, she reported that there was a very large cake on the table and she assumed that perhaps it was someone's birthday. "They are all drinking and eating a lot," she said.

"Nothing wrong with that, is there?" asked Flapper.

"No, I don't think so. In fact, they seem to be happy," said Woody with a curious tone in his voice. "Maybe we have found the Happiness Bug, or at least we have found the place where people come to be happy."

Everyone fell silent, thinking about what Woody had just said. The people down below were getting louder and louder. The laughter had a shrill, almost unnatural sound to it and some people were walking around as if they could no longer stand up straight. Others were consuming what seemed like mountains of food. One woman was eating her third helping of birthday cake, while a man at her side was having his second helping of hamburgers. Vast quantities of liquid refreshment seemed to be contributing to the loudness of the party. Other people, who were not drinking, were rushing around clearing up and generally tending to other people's needs.

"Is this consumption of food and liquid what people call having a good time?" asked Mrs. Blue Jay innocently.

"That's what I am wondering, too," said Woody.

"I think it's all right to eat, drink and be merry. Being with friends and sharing good times and lots of laughter is healthy and I have heard Amethyst speak of such things, but it is the excessive consumption that strikes me as problematic," he continued. "Why do they feel the need to eat and drink so much?"

"Well!" said Woody in a voice that the told the others he was about to declare a profoundly simplistic truth. "We are in the State of Addiction, are we not? I would think that what we are witnessing is not exactly happiness, but addictive behaviors such as over-eating, drinking too much happy juice and a chronic dose of workaholism."

"Why are they unhappy? What are they avoiding?"

"I don't know Flapper," said Woody, "but we seem to be getting further and further away from the Happiness Bug. We seem to be finding sources of unhappiness and avoidance and that is not what Amethyst sent us to find. I am afraid we are going to let her down and we will be going home to tell her that the Happiness Bug is indeed missing."

"Come and see what is happening over here," said Mr. Blue Jay, who had been out exploring while the others were talking.

They all flew over to join him. There was a large group of children, some standing, some sitting and some cowering in corners, but all of them were crying and apparently hurting in some way.

"I cannot figure it out," said Mr. Blue Jay. "It is very distressing. They are in the same park as the adults, the adults can see them, can see that they are crying and hurting and yet they seem to be ignoring them. And equally strange, is the fact that the children are not running to the adults asking for help."

As the birds watched this incredible sight, the laughter from the adults got louder and louder and the sobbing from the children became quieter and quieter, fading almost to nothing.

"Let's move on and give ourselves time to think about what we have seen. Perhaps it will make sense later," said Woody as the four friends took off in a northeasterly direction.

Later that day they arrived in the State of Reality and alighted on a tree in the Village Square. They saw an older couple sitting below them on an oak bench. They were watching people passing by and almost everyone stopped and talked to the couple.

THE VILLAGE OF ILLUSIONS

"I have an idea," said Woody. "It seems to me that the couple on the bench knows almost everyone who passes them and I just overheard the woman complaining about how unhappy everyone is and saying that perhaps they had lost something. I think we need to ask them to help us."

"How can we do that, Woody?" exclaimed Flapper in an incredulous tone.

"I am not sure, but let's follow them for a while and see what happens," offered Woody, having no better suggestion. The four friends followed Sam and Sally Spectator all day, watching them speaking to people in the Village Square, having lunch, taking Mrs. Rover for groceries and then walking her home before they headed home themselves. By the time, they reached Sam and Sally's home, Woody was convinced that Sally Spectator was going to be very helpful to them. He liked her intuition and her compassion. As they sat on a branch of the tree in their driveway, he saw Sally look back at them as Sam opened their front door. Tomorrow they would devise a plan to get Sally and Sam to help them. For tonight, however, they had better get some rest.

Sally awakened to the noise of the birds outside of their bedroom window. "Listen to the birds, Sam. I have never heard them twittering so loudly, almost as if they are calling to us," said Sally.

"Don't be so foolish, woman, birds don't call to humans. But you are right about one thing, they are making a fine racket out there."

"It is time to get up anyway. Let's go downstairs and have some breakfast. I'll brew the coffee if you make the eggs. You really are the best at cooking eggs," said Sally, laughing.

Sam smiled, knowing that Sally's acknowledgement of his egg-cooking prowess was a show of affection. After all, it was impossible to live with someone for many years and not have cultivated some little sparring matches, which were really a manifestation of the core strength and warmth of the relationship. A casual onlooker might misinterpret the intentions, but Sally and Sam knew the real stories behind their banter.

While Sam was cooking breakfast, Sally ventured out into the garden to tend to her roses and to water the plants. As she was watering the roses, she heard a voice. "Hello, Sally, we need to talk to you."

Sally looked around. She could see no one.

"Hello. Over here," a voice said.

She looked around again. Still no one, only a couple of birds perched on a nearby branch. I must have had one glass of sherry too many last night, thought Sally. The morning dove flew from the branch and perched on the roof of Sally's car.

"Over here, Sally," he exclaimed, feeling a trifle frustrated that she was not taking him seriously.

"Well, I never," Sally exclaimed. "A talking bird. Now I know I had too much to drink last night!"

"Good morning, Sally. My name is Woody, and this is my cousin Flapper and Mr. & Mrs. Blue Jay," said Woody.

It was hard to measure the incredulity that Sally was now feeling. Either she had completely lost her marbles or she was having a very senior moment.

"Good morning, Woody, nice to meet you," she said tentatively, never having spoken to a morning dove before.

"We heard you talking yesterday about how unhappy people have become and how you think they have lost something. We have been sent by Princess Amethyst to look for the Happiness Bug because she also believes that the people in the State of Reality have lost it. So, given your wonderful insights, we were wondering if we could enlist your help."

"Gosh, Woody," said Sally, suddenly becoming shy and demure. She did not know whether to be flattered or continue being astonished. "I would be honored to help, but how can I do that and who is Princess Amethyst?"

Woody explained all about Amethyst and the Island State of Inner Wisdom as Sally listened, wide-eyed in amazement. She had always intuitively known there was more to life than just the daily grind and this was the confirmation. We are here for a reason, she thought; we have to find out life's purpose and it is our job to grow and develop.

Just at that moment, Sam came into the garden looking for Sally. She had been gone for some time and he was getting worried about her, not to mention the fact that he was hungry and ready for breakfast.

"Sally, where are you?" he called.

"Over here, Sam, I'm talking to the birds."

Oh, boy! It is going to be one of those days, thought Sam. Sometimes Sally's way of thinking about the world was a bit further on the edge than Sam was comfortable with, but he did love her, so he tried his best to understand where she was coming from. Today was going to be no exception. She was his best friend and he could not imagine ever living without her, but sometimes she stretched his limits. He walked towards her with a skeptical look on his face and much to his astonishment he could hear the birds talking, too.

"We are not sure how you can help, but we thought if we did this together that having more brains on the job might be useful. In any case we have bird brains and you have the same kind of brains as the people

THE VILLAGE OF ILLUSIONS

who have lost the Happiness Bug, so we just thought that perhaps you could help us to think this through," said Mrs. Blue Jay.

Sally quickly brought Sam up to speed. "Let's go and have some breakfast and talk this over," said Sam, in part, because he was hungry, but also because he needed time to think.

"OK, Sam. Woody, you all wait here and we will be back shortly," said Sally to her new friends.

After breakfast, Sally and Sam appeared back in the garden where the birds were waiting anxiously.

"Well, Woody, we have talked this over and have both agreed that you are on a very important mission and we would be honored to help in whatever way we can," said Sally.

The birds were delighted and flew around the garden in a victory celebration.

"I have been thinking about this," said Sally. "I'm not sure if this is a good lead, but there is a wise old owl that lives on the edge of Discovery Forest, which is just on the edge of the State of Reality. It is quite a long way, but it might be worth the trip."

"What an excellent idea," exclaimed Woody. "Now why didn't we think of that? You see, it was a good idea to expand our team and allow for some diversity of thinking. We are sometimes too close to the situation and don't always see the forest from the trees."

Sam and Sally went back indoors to pack for their adventure, returning wearing comfortable shoes and carrying backpacks full of essential goodies such as water, light-weight rain gear, a flashlight and, of course, sandwiches. What an unlikely team they made, but everyone was happy at the prospect of working together. The birds could have made it to the wise old owl's house much faster without Sally and Sam, but out of respect for them, they just flew overhead, circling as they did so, in order to keep pace.

They soon arrived at the forest and walked through to a clearing that the locals called Owl Hollow. Sam and Sally started calling for Mr. Owl.

"What is all the noise about?" said Mr. Owl, startled from his daytime sleep. "Don't you people know that I sleep during the day and only work at night?"

"Yes, I am sorry, Mr. Owl. We really do know that, but we have a big problem and we need your help, but first, let me introduce you to our new friends." Sally introduced Woody and his friends to Mr. Owl.

Owls possess silent wisdom and healing powers and have the ability to see what others cannot. (Andrews 2001, p.173).

Helen Turnbull, Ph. D.

"It is very nice to meet all of you, now let's go over and sit down in my meeting area and we can talk about this dilemma of yours."

They all went over to an opening in the hollow where there was a large stump from an oak tree that Sam and Sally sat on. Mr. Owl flew on to a very large swing attached to the oak tree with two large pieces of rope. He wrapped his wings around the ropes and began to swing gently while he waited for the others to settle down. The four birds perched on a low branch of a bush. The group had managed to form a circle. "Go ahead, tell me your story," said Mr. Owl.

Everyone began speaking at once.

"One at a time, please. After all, I am not a morning bird. You can't all chatter at once and expect me to digest what you are saying."

The group looked at each other and then deferred to Woody to start the story.

"Well, where do I begin? I guess at the beginning," said Woody pragmatically.

"You see, Mr. Owl, we, I mean the birds, we live on the Island State of Inner Wisdom. Amethyst, who is the guardian of Inner Wisdom, is very worried that the people in the State of Reality have somehow lost the ability to be happy, and she thinks that must mean that the Happiness Bug is missing. So, she sent us to find her."

At this point Sally jumped in to the conversation.

"I was saying to Sam just the other day that I felt people are less happy than they used to be. I might not have called it the Happiness Bug, but it's as good a name as any for the dilemma," she concluded.

"Hmm!" said Mr. Owl, rubbing his chin, a habit that wise people seem to have. "And where have you been looking for this elusive Happiness Bug?"

It was Mrs. Blue Jay's turn to jump into the conversation.

"We have been all over. We went to the State of Worthiness, the City of Productivity, the State of Recreation and Relaxation, the State of Esteem, the State of Addictions, and the State of Reality."

This was all news to Sam and Sally, too, so everyone listened intently.

"These are all good places to visit," said Mr. Owl, nodding approvingly. "What did you find out when you were there?"

Flapper got in on the action this time.

"Ah! We found out lots of things and we may have some pieces of the puzzle, but we certainly don't have the answer," he said.

"Well, try me," said Mr. Owl. "Let's hear what you have learned already and it just might give us a clue about where to look next."

"We went to the State of Worthiness first and there we learned that people like to be busy and to feel productive. They like to feel empowered by their work, but they do not like to work for people who bully them. We also learned that they collect a lot of baggage and they need to learn to leave it at the door, but we think that may not be so easy for them," said Flapper.

"Ah, now that is interesting," said Sally. "That is exactly what I have been worrying about. I think it is true that people like to be busy and productive, but I think it is also possible to be too busy and that causes stress. Everyone rushes around, leaving no time for themselves or other people," she added.

"As for the baggage part, you are right there also. The problem with baggage is that some of it is so old that people don't even realize they are carrying it anymore," added Sam. "And if you don't know you are carrying it, how can you know to leave it at the door?"

"Where did you go then?" asked Mr. Owl.

"We went to the State of Recreation and Relaxation," said Mr. Blue Jay, "where we learned a lot of things. We learned that people like to be in beautiful places. They like the sunshine and they like the warm wind in their faces. They like the sense of freedom they get from doing something they want to do and they like to be spontaneous. They like laughter and they like to be with family and friends."

"They like the safety and security they feel from being with people they love," said Mrs. Blue Jay, joining in the conversation.

"That is a very long list," said Mr. Owl.

"Oh, and one more thing, being on holiday means there is a sense of escaping from the normal daily routines and commitments," added Mr. Blue Jay.

"It is very good to be on vacation," said Sally. "People manage to recharge their batteries and even the most grumpy citizen comes back feeling refreshed. Trouble is that people today are so busy rushing around that they seem to think that a long weekend is a vacation. That is not enough time to let you regain your lost energy."

Thinking about grumpy people reminded Mrs. Blue Jay of something. "Oh, yes, and then we went to the State of Esteem, where people were exercising and working out. It seemed like they were doing it to get rid of baggage and stress. People kept talking about what an awful day they had had and how the people they worked with were unpleasant."

Sam thought about this for a moment and then interjected, "Sometimes people are working out just to stay healthy, to lose weight and to keep their bodies in shape, not because they don't like their work colleagues," he said.

"That may be true, Sam, but we are just telling you what we heard people saying," said Mr. Blue Jay, feeling he should defend Mrs. Blue Jay.

Sensing a little tension, the group became quiet and they all turned to Mr. Owl, looking to him to make sense of the situation.

Mr. Owl thought for a few minutes and then pronounced, "Actually, you are both correct. You see, people who exercise are doing so in order to keep fit and at the same time they know that it helps them manage their stress." He paused for a moment and then went on to say, "And... people who feel stressed know that exercising will help them to relieve the tension. In addition, I think there are people who just like to complain, even when they are having a good day. So you see, you are both correct," he said with a smile.

Everyone immediately relaxed.

"So, where did you go next?" Mr. Owl asked, sensing that the group was ready to move on to another topic.

"Ah, this one was the most difficult of all," said Woody. "We went to the State of Addictions, where we found people enjoying themselves, drinking and eating. There was lots of laughter and yet we came away with an uneasy feeling. There were a couple of strange factors, which we confess we still do not fully understand. First, there was the laughter; it got louder and louder and yet something was not quite right. Second, there were children crying in the corner and all of the adults were ignoring them."

"Ah! That is troubling. What do you think it might have meant?" asked Mr. Owl with a quizzical look.

The group fell unusually silent as everyone thought about the question.

After some time Sally was the first to break the silence. "Well, I think it means that when an enjoyment becomes excessive it is no longer really an enjoyment. People may start out doing something because it's social, like eating or drinking, but when it becomes excessive...," her voice trailed off as she sensed the judgment in her statement.

"I think you are right, Sally," said Sam supportively.

"Why do you think the children were being ignored in the corner?" asked Mr. Owl.

Everyone looked at each other and after a long pause Mrs. Blue Jay said, "I think I know what it means, but I have been reluctant to share my thoughts in case you thought I was being stupid."

THE VILLAGE OF ILLUSIONS

"There are no stupid thoughts here, Mrs. Blue Jay, please go ahead," said Mr. Owl.

"OK then, I will. Thank you. I think that the children represented the inner child for each of the adults. It was almost as if the adults had become numb and were eating or drinking in order to avoid their own pain."

Everyone stared at Mrs. Blue Jay for a few minutes, letting what she had just said sink in.

Her husband broke the silence. "Oh, my dear, you are so smart," said Mr. Blue Jay. "You are always underestimating your own abilities and your powers of observation. You should share your thoughts more often."

Mrs. Blue Jay smiled demurely, secretly pleased to have her husband acknowledge her in this way.

"That is an interesting observation indeed," said Mr. Owl. "Do you think that is why the Happiness Bug is lost? Because people are in pain and doing everything they can to avoid it?"

"Well, it could be one of the reasons. Maybe they are not deliberately avoiding it. They are just no longer in touch with the things that have hurt them. Perhaps they have developed negative patterns of behavior without realizing it," Mrs. Blue Jay answered, anxious to defend her argument.

"You have all had quite a journey so far, and have certainly given me a lot to think about," said Mr. Owl. "I'll tell you what, when I have a lot on my mind I like to go for a trip through the woods; just fly around and take in all the wonderful nature around me." He hesitated for a second, then laughed. In deference to Sam and Sally he said, "In your case there will be no flying. Let's go for a walk through Discovery Forest."

The group set off down the path, which led them further into the forest. As they were walking, they heard a noise in front of them and suddenly animals and insects surrounded them, all looking like they were in an incredible hurry.

"What is wrong?" asked Woody. "Where are you all rushing to?"

Puffing and panting, one of the rabbits stopped long enough to say, "It's not what we are rushing TO that is the question, it's what we are rushing FROM!" He hurried on his way.

"Wait a minute," called Woody. "What are you rushing from?"

The rabbit looked back over his tail and said, "A giant bug! It's stomping around the forest in a state of anxiety and looks like it's lost. It's so large that we are afraid it's going to stomp on all of us, so we cleared out as fast as we could."

The friends all looked at each other. A giant bug! Could this be the Happiness Bug they were seeking? What was it doing stomping around and scaring everyone else out of the forest?

"Let's go and find out what is happening," said Mr. Owl.

Sam and Sally proceeded tentatively. The shortness of their steps reflected their increasing anxiety at the prospect of meeting up with a giant bug. All of the forest animals were afraid. They were heading out of the forest. Perhaps that is where they should be heading? The birds circled slowly overhead, also reluctant to reach their new destination. They could hear scuffling and Mr. Owl told them all to slow down and gather behind a large oak tree.

"I think perhaps one of us should fly over and find out how big the bug really is and report back to the others," suggested Mrs. Blue Jay.

"Good idea, Mrs. Blue Jay. Who wants to volunteer?" asked Mr. Owl.

"I'll go," said Flapper bravely.

"OK, thanks. Do not get into any encounters with the bug. Just fly high overhead and come back and tell us what you see," instructed Mr. Owl.

Flapper took off and the others waited breathlessly for his return. A pregnant silence fell over the group as they reflected on their journey and wondered what was going to happen next. Somehow they had not anticipated feeling anxious about meeting the Happiness Bug, if indeed that was who they were about to confront.

Flapper returned to report that there was indeed a very large bug stomping around the forest. He told the others that the bug looked agitated and lost and was scuffling around in the undergrowth as if it were looking for something.

"Does he look dangerous?" asked Sally nervously.

"Actually, it looks like a giant ladybug, but I'm not sure. It is purple with yellow spots. No, it does not look dangerous. Maybe just lost and scared," said Flapper thoughtfully.

"Oh, I like ladybugs. Everyone likes ladybugs. Do you think we should all go and try to help? I mean, even if it is not actually the Happiness Bug, it is certainly causing some chaos in the forest and maybe needs help," said Sally, who was often filled with compassion for others in need.

Everyone nodded in agreement. They began to ease closer to where the ladybug was. Sally gasped and jumped two steps back.

"It is pretty big. Bigger than I expected," said Sally.

"One of us needs to approach it. Who do you think it should be?" Sam added, hoping it was not to be him.

Mr. Owl spoke up and told the group that he thought, as he was the appointed leader of this crew, that he should be the one to step forward at a moment like this. Everyone was grateful and relieved that he was willing to assume that level of leadership and display that amount of courage.

Mr. Owl flew onto a nearby tree just in front of the ladybug. "Hello, Ladybug. How are you today?"

"Oh! Hello, Mr. Owl. Everyone else is running away from me, so why are you here?" the ladybug inquired with a sad tone.

"Yes, I noticed that everyone is running in the opposite direction, but I am not sure that they understand why they are running. I thought I would find out who you are; ask you if you need help and if there is a reason for everyone to be so afraid of you."

The ladybug stopped scuffling and sat down. "I don't know where to go. No one takes me seriously and everyone here seems to be afraid of me."

"Do you mind if my friends join us?"

"No, of course not," said Ladybug, wondering if perhaps she was finally going to be able to tell her story.

Helen Turnbull, Ph. D.

THE HAPPINESS BUG

THE VILLAGE OF ILLUSIONS

Mr. Owl beckoned the others to come out from behind the trees. Everyone settled down at a polite but safe distance from the large ladybug and began to listen. Mr. Owl introduced everyone and Ladybug said she was delighted to meet everyone.

"Do you mind if I ask you... are you in fact a ladybug? You look like one, but you have different colors. Where are you actually from?" asked Woody.

"Yes, I am a ladybug. I am a very special ladybug. In fact, I am the Queen of the ladybugs and I have a very exceptional job. That is why my colors are so vibrant and unique. I live in the State of Reality, but I am not visible very often. My cousins are seen all the time." Ladybug hesitated for a second. "Well, my male cousins are seen all the time, that is. They are red with black dots and everyone notices them. My female cousins are brown with no dots and no one seems to see them. They do all of the work and are overlooked and taken for granted, almost in the same way that people overlook all the positive things in their lives."

The group fell silent, taking in the enormity of what Ladybug had just said.

"What happened? Why are you so lost?" queried Mr. Owl, wondering whether they had really discovered the elusive Happiness Bug, but feeling it was not the right time to ask that question.

"I did not GET lost. I left. I feel lost because I don't know what to do next, but I left because I did not feel I was appreciated," she said.

"You seem so sad and anxious. What was it that caused you to not feel needed?" asked Mr. Owl.

Ladybug sighed deeply and started to speak. "I feel useless and unwanted. It just seems to me that people would rather do anything else than pay attention to me. They are all so busy, filling their lives with noise and activity and never taking time for themselves or each other."

"Oh dear, that sounds so sad. Are you sure things are that bad?" asked Sally.

"Yes, I am sure. People would much rather be miserable than be happy these days," said Ladybug, with a note of despair in her voice.

There was a stunned silence in the group as everyone realized that they probably had found the Happiness Bug. Woody broke the silence.

"Are you...are you by any chance the Happiness Bug?" he asked, his voice quivering.

"Yes, but you wouldn't think it to look at me. I am the unhappiest Happiness Bug you will ever meet."

"I know it is not a polite question to ask a ladybug," said Mr. Owl, clearing his throat, "but I would like to ask you another question." He took a deep breath. "Why are you so large?"

"You're right, it is not a polite question, but I understand why you are asking it. I am not supposed to be this large, but the more unhappy and unloved I felt, the more I ate. I just ate and ate until one day I realized I had become too large to be lovable. That felt like a vicious circle, but it was too late. Now in order to return to my normal size, I need to rediscover my own happiness and sense of purpose. I thought I would leave in search of happiness. There is another country where the Queen has a National Happiness Measurement. She works to ensure that her people are happy. I thought I might try to find that country and live there, where I might be more useful. Then perhaps I can find myself again. Of one thing I am clear; if I am not happy I cannot help others to be happy."

The group fell silent for a few minutes.

"I am quite depressed by what you say," said Sally. "It makes me very sad to think of you, above all, losing your happiness. If you are not happy, there is no chance for the rest of us. I have been worried about people in our Village of Illusions. They do not seem happy anymore. I hope you do not leave, because we really do need you. We just don't always know it."

"What is that expression? If you don't use it, you lose it," said Sam. "Yes, that's it, we have forgotten how to use it, and now you are thinking of leaving us. Oh, dear..." his voice tapered off as he took in the vastness of that possibility.

The birds became silent witnesses as they realized that they had done their job in finding the Happiness Bug. It was really a matter for the people in the State of Reality, represented here by Sam and Sally to figure out if they valued happiness enough to work for its return.

Ladybug had been listening intently to the conversation. "Some people have held me in the palm of their hands and just flicked me away. Others seem intent on being miserable and remaining miserable and they do not even see me at all. Sometimes they even step on me without noticing. Then there are people who used to talk to me all the time and now they do not want to know me. It is almost as if people do not think they deserve to be happy. The entire society seems made up of bad news. People watch the news to hear what bad things happened today. The good news comes at the end, by which time no one is listening. If someone laughs too much I hear people saying, 'what are you so happy about? There must be something wrong with you. It is not natural to be that cheerful.'"

She sighed deeply and then continued. "I don't get it, really. Is it not better to have a happy disposition than a sad one?" Almost as if that were a rhetorical statement she added, "You know, when you are negative you draw negative energy to you. I notice that people who spend their day complaining always seem to get what they ask for. If we emitted happy energy, we might be surprised by what comes back to us. People are living in fear today. They are scared and being scared is not a happy place to live. Look at me, for example, all of the birds and the animals were scared and running away from me because I am no longer happy. When I am happy, everyone wants to be around me. I once heard that someone wanted to introduce a Gross National Happiness Indicator and that the idea was squashed like a bug. I suppose they would rather have a Gross National Misery Indicator. Maybe they make more money from people being miserable. Being miserable makes people sick," she said, somewhat philosophically. "I'm sorry, I am rambling, I know, but it has been so long since I felt anyone would listen to me. It is good to talk."

"Gosh, Ladybug, everything you say makes perfect sense to me. You are right. We are so busy rushing around and it does seem that we place more value on negative stories. Perhaps we have forgotten how to be happy," said Sally. "After all, just look at the news and the expression, 'no news is good news.'"

Sam had been sitting, rubbing his chin and looking very pensive. "What would it take to persuade you to come back and give us a second chance?" "Happiness is a state of mind, Sam," said Ladybug. "It is about making a conscious choice each day to view your world from a positive frame of reference. It does not mean I want people to be happy all the time. That is not even possible, but I would like people to be more upbeat and positive about their lives. Maybe if they consumed less sugar… oh well, that's another story." She hesitated for a few moments, contemplating her next statement. "If I thought that people would be willing to work on having a happy disposition, or at least a happier disposition, then I would be willing to come back." For the first time since they met, Ladybug began to smile and then she began to laugh. "The truth is I didn't really want to leave. The State of Reality is the only home I have ever known, but I didn't know what else to do."

"I have an idea," said Sally. Her mind had been working overtime while she was listening to Ladybug's story. "What if we started Happiness meetings at the Village Hall? That would be a good place to start, helping people to talk about happiness. We could use the ladybug as our symbol and we could create little Happiness Pods, groups who meet together and learn more about becoming happy."

"I like that idea, Sally," said Sam, "but do you really think people will come?"

"I don't know, Sam, but we can try. You and I will be there, right?"

"Yes, of course," said Sam, affirming her suggestion.

"Well, that's a good start then. If we go, others will follow and our positive energy will draw others to us," said Sally with more conviction than she had felt in years.

"Where will you live in the State of Reality, Ladybug... if you agree to come back, I mean?" asked Sam.

"Ah, I live everywhere. When you see one of my cousins, it is a positive sign that you are surrounded by happiness. The positive energies emanating from inside all of you give me the oxygen to continue. Having a happy disposition can help you to move mountains. If the entire country became happier, we could even positively affect other countries," Ladybug announced, feeling much happier than she had at the beginning of the day. The thought of going home again and of being wanted filled her with great contentment.

There was a loud round of applause and as she looked up, she realized that while she had been telling her story, all of the animals, birds and insects had come back into the forest and had been listening to her story.

"What a journey we have had together," said Woody as they said adieu to their new friends, Mr. Owl and Sally and Sam. Sally and Sam were heading back home, intent on starting up their Happiness meetings. Mr. Owl was heading back to catch up on some lost sleep, as he felt certain his wisdom would be needed another day. Ladybug was already on her way back to the State of Reality and now it was time for Woody, Flapper, and Mr. and Mrs. Blue Jay to fly back to Inner Wisdom. They knew that Amethyst would be thrilled when they

"I hope we meet again, Woody," Sally said, somewhat wistfully. She was going to miss her new friends. It had been an enormous adventure. It had seemed surreal and yet she knew that it was a privilege to be able to communicate with the birds and to play a part in such an important project.

"I hope so, too, Sally. Until we do, just remember that every time you see a blue jay or a morning dove, even if it is not one of us, it is the essence of us and we will be sending you our good wishes," said Woody.

With that, the birds spread their wings and headed back in the direction of the Island State of Inner Wisdom.

Patience was sobbing as she sat next to Amethyst. "Oh wow! Amethyst, you really know what stories to pick. This story really hits the spot. I am not happy. So much has happened to me over the years and I feel so defensive and protective that I think I have lost the ability to be happy. I stay angry most of the time and I live in a state of constant anxiety and fear. I feel fearful that the people who hurt me will do it again, anger that I let it happen and anxiety that I might not have learned from my mistakes and might let new people in my life treat me badly also. I seem unable to let my defenses down and I do not like myself anymore. I used to be a nice person, but I have lost touch with the person I used to be, I think I am frozen in a very negative state," said Patience through her tears.

Handing Patience a lace handkerchief to dry her tears, Amethyst said, "It will be OK, Patience. I know it does not feel like it, but you are already on the road back. Let's go to the last story for this evening."

Chapter Nine
Arctic of Ice Valley

Mental models come in two varieties – those that make life more difficult by leading to stuck situations and those that make life easier by solving problems.
(O'Connor and McDermott 1997)

Golden Threads and Silver Needles:

Amethyst was delighted at such a hopeful and positive outcome to the story of the Happiness Bug. She could not help but wonder what makes people adopt an unhappy demeanor such that they are in danger of losing sight of happiness altogether.

She knew that each tree on Inner Wisdom Avenue carried incredible wisdom and knowledge and held the stories of the many ways in which people could become stuck on their journey towards happiness. Patience had said she felt she was living in a frozen state and Amethyst knew there was a story in one of the libraries that would be perfect for her. She stopped at an enormous tree, pushed aside the golden threads and put her hand on the anchor, which slowly moved aside and revealed a door that took her inside the tree. The interior housed a most abundant and luxurious library with shelves that were filled with very grand leather books. She walked with purpose straight over to the shelf that she knew contained the story she was seeking.

"Ah! This is it. This one is for Patience," she said as she made her way back outside.

THE VILLAGE OF ILLUSIONS

She carefully carried the book to the wrought-iron bench outside, and with Patience by her side, once again invoked the wisdom of the silver needle.

Arctic lived in Ice Valley. Not surprisingly, it was a very cold place, but Arctic was used to that. She had not lived there all of her life, but she had spent a considerable number of years there and had become accustomed to the climate. She was not quite sure how she arrived there or indeed why she chose to live in such a cold place.

One would think that in a place so cold, people would have worked out how to get warm, but that was not the case in Ice Valley. Arctic and all the other residents stayed perpetually cold. She had a vague recollection that there was a time in her life when she had been much warmer, but she could not really remember what it was like or how to get back there.

On this particular day, she was walking through the town on her way down to the harbor to buy some lobster for dinner when she noticed a path she had not seen before. She was curious. Where could that be leading? she wondered.

She looked at her watch. Did she have time to take a side trip? Why not, what do I have to lose? There is a kind of drudgery to being stuck in Ice Valley. She thought it would be an adventure to explore new places, so she set off down the path. She was equipped with protective clothing and very good ice-walking shoes; nevertheless, she needed to be careful on this path as it was particularly icy. She proceeded tentatively, wishing she had brought someone else along for company. She intuitively knew, however, that this journey was best undertaken alone.

She came to a signpost with some long icicles dangling from it. There was only one direction on the signpost. It said "Rejection." She was puzzled and yet she thought it seemed strangely familiar to her. As she stood there, the icicles began tinkling in the breeze. How odd! Icicles do not move, she thought. They were moving and bumping against each other as if they were a wind chime blowing in the cold breeze. As she watched, one of the icicles transformed itself into a golden thread and, as if it were melting off the signpost, fell to the ground and began to move forward down the path. When the astonished Arctic did not follow, the thread stopped and waited a few moments. Arctic remained motionless with fear. . The thread seemed to get tired of waiting and in an agitated movement, which only a frozen thread can do, it spun itself into a sphere, flew off the ground and motioned for her to follow. Arctic began walking quickly. She threaded her way carefully down the icy path, going deeper into the woodlands.

Suddenly she heard a movement and someone shouted, "Stop, don't come any closer!"

THE VILLAGE OF ILLUSIONS

ANONYMOUS SNOWMAN

Arctic gasped and jumped back. She was quite startled to meet anyone as it seemed so cold and unwelcoming in the woods, but she was even less prepared to be confronting a talking snowman. The snowman was standing guard holding an ice bayonet across his chest and clearly taking his job very seriously.

"*Don't come any closer,*" *he warned her again.*

She looked over and noticed that the thread seemed to be taking a seat on the nearest wall, waiting, almost in anticipation.

"*Hello, Mr. Snowman,*" *Arctic said, in the hope that his heart would melt a little in her direction.* "*My name is Arctic, what is yours?*"

The snowman looked confused. "*I don't have a name. I am not that important. My only purpose is to guard this tree,*" *he said.*

"*Well, you are doing a very fine job of that,*" *Arctic said.* "*But what is so important about this tree?*"

"*That's just it. I don't really know, but the people who use it are really invested in having it stay just the way it is,*" *said the snowman.*

Arctic became more curious. What importance could this tree possibly have that it had to have an anonymous snowman guarding it? Suddenly, the frozen thread slid from its seat on the wall and grabbed her by the hand, pulling her towards another path. She waved goodbye to the snowman, wishing she could have gotten to know him better. He seemed like a well-intentioned snowman and it was a pity he did not even know his own name or why he was stuck there guarding a frozen tree.

The thread led Arctic down a path, which wound its way round to the back of the tree. At the base of the tree, there was a set of stairs leading down to the inside of it. How strange! But then again, this entire trip was strange and not one she had anticipated taking when she set off earlier that day.

As she walked up into the tree, she noticed that there were little sets of steps leading up to each of the branches. The steps were not large enough to put your entire foot on them, but you could delicately put your toes on them. She looked towards the thread for directions, but thread had taken a seat at the base of the tree and was looking non-committal, as if it were telling her, "*It is up to you. I got you here, you choose! Stay, go, left, right, you are on your own!*"

Whatever! She randomly selected a set of steps to climb. She

THE VILLAGE OF ILLUSIONS

found herself moving into a very wide branch that had lots of little shoots and entrails hanging down. It was a bizarre experience being on the inside of a tree branch. There were many knots on the branch and she found one that actually had a hole in it, enabling her to not only look outside, but also reach outside. As she peered out, she saw what looked like a Christmas tree bauble hanging from one of the small tributary branches. She reached through the hole and gently pulled it towards her. It was a frosted glass bottle. She rubbed at the bottle to remove the frost and inside she saw a squirrel. She slowly took the top off the bottle and much to her astonishment the squirrel started moving. She put the bottle on the ground and the squirrel wriggled his way out of it.

"Well, thank goodness and about time, too. I wondered if anyone was ever going to rescue me," exclaimed the very irritated squirrel. "What took you so long?"

Arctic could not quite figure out which emotion took precedence, her amazement at revealing a talking squirrel or her defensiveness at the blame he was assigning.

"Mr. Squirrel," she exclaimed, quite indignantly, "your predicament has absolutely nothing to do with me. In fact, I think you should be more grateful. After all, I have just rescued you."

"Rescued me? Rescued me? You people are all the same, never taking responsibility for your actions," said the squirrel. "Come with me," he said quickly, before Arctic had a chance to protest..

"Before I got stuck in that bottle, I dedicated my life to scurrying and planning and preparing, and I have been preparing for the arrival of a Stucky for a very long time," said the squirrel as he bustled his way back down the steps.

"A Stucky? What is a Stucky and to whom are you referring to when you say 'you people'? My name is Arctic and I live in Ice Valley," she said, her indignation at him growing by the minute. The squirrel was moving over to another branch and beginning to climb the steps.

"Come on, slow poke! Honestly! You move like molasses!" he said, chastising Arctic for taking so long to follow him.

"No! Not another step until you tell me what a Stucky is. Who are you? Why were you stuck in that bottle and why are you being so insulting to me," she demanded.

The squirrel stopped and looked back at her, rubbing his chin as he thought about her protestations. She seemed quite serious, so he figured he had better explain something in order to get her moving again.

"Oh, very well then, but let's make this quick. We have important work to do. With a quick flick of his very furry tail, he sat down and began to explain. "Those of us in Frozen Forest call all of the people who live in Ice Valley 'Stuckies' because they have all adopted behaviors and defenses which may have served them well at one time, but do not continue to serve them well. Because they have been hurt in the past, they have built defensive walls that are so high that they no longer recognize themselves. Their behavior quite often has a negative impact on others, but they seem unable to stop themselves, like a runaway train, if you know what I mean. The coldness of their behavior keeps them in a frozen state and ensures that they keep others at a distance. It is good to have defenses; it is a good coping strategy. But," said the squirrel with a long pause for effect, "when a coping mechanism is overused, or gets stuck in a groove (if you will forgive the pun), then it is harmful to the individual. Hatred harms the host, can't you see that? You see, everyone at Ice Valley is stuck or frozen into a form of behavior that is no longer in their best interest.

"OK, have I said enough? Can we continue?" asked the squirrel. "Oh, and I almost forgot," he said, extending one of his paws in Arctic's direction. "I'm Stasher, nice to meet you."

While a large part of Arctic wanted to stomp out of the tree base, assuming she could have found her way home, another part of her recognized some truth in what the squirrel had just said. \Somewhere in the distance she could hear the sounds of a wind chime, almost as if it was ringing in a message from her soul. She had long believed she was stuck in Ice Valley, she just did not know why.

"OK, that explains some of it, but why were you stuck in a frozen bottle waiting for me to release you?"

Stasher sat down on the steps and for a moment looked quite dejected. "Huh! I suppose that is not an unreasonable question. OK then, I will explain. I was confined to the bottle as punishment for being selfish, stashing too much stuff and being greedy. I was not looking out for others and merely stashing as much as I could for myself. The council of squirrels had a meeting and decided that they would stash me in that bottle until a Stucky came along and released me and then it would be my job to help the Stucky to become unstuck. I guess what goes around comes around. I owe you and you owe me! OK. Have I told you enough? Are you ready to come with me? I cannot have total liberty unless I help you, so are you willing to cooperate? Then we can both be on our road to freedom. What do you say?" said Stasher with an anxious tone in his voice.

Arctic thought about what Stasher had said. On the one hand, it sounded preposterous and at the same time, she felt powerless to resist following him.

"There is something of a paradox in the fact that you tell me that your punishment was for your selfishness and yet I sense that your motivation for helping me is also selfish. I guess everyone has an agenda. However, as I do believe it might also be to my advantage, let us just be selfish together. OK, Stasher, you have a deal. Let's go," she said, much to Stasher's relief.

The Stucky Museum:

Stasher led Arctic up another set of stairs, this time to a narrow pathway with a sign that said "Rut Road." This road had many smaller trails leading off in many different directions. There was Furrow Lane, Deep Trouble Terrace and Low Mood Court. Arctic could only imagine what she would find down these roads if she had the chance to explore them. Stasher continued to lead her down Rut Road and they came to a large building with an imposing entranceway. It had columns on either side of a staircase and as Arctic looked up she saw the sign across the door that said, "Main Branch, Stucky Museum."

Well, this should be a treat! Just what I need. A walk through a museum. I don't even like museums, thought Arctic.

They walked up to the front desk. The museum curator, who was a Badger, greeted them.

"Hello, hello," he said. "What do we have here?"

The squirrel laughed and said, "This is Arctic, she is a Stucky from Ice Valley and I would like you to give us a tour of the museum."

"Oh, very well then, come along with me," said the badger, immediately busying himself with preparation for the official tour.

Professor Badger did not get the chance to give too many tours, especially to Stuckies, as most people avoided this branch of the museum for fear of contamination, and certainly, it was a rare event when a Stucky ventured past. This was a treat indeed and he was going to enjoy showing Arctic around.

Before they set off on their tour, Stasher pulled Arctic aside and told her about badgers. He told her that when a badger comes into your life it is a sign that you should dig deeper and get beneath the surface of your behaviors. It is time to tell a new story about yourself and your life. (Andrews 2001).

They set off on their tour, making strange bedfellows, a squirrel, a badger and a Stucky. As they walked into the first main room of the museum, they saw a large bronze statue. There were two androgynous people; one figure was standing with arms outstretched, like the branches of a tree, with a monkey clinging tightly to his back. In between the two people there was another monkey suspended in mid air. The second person was twisting around in a motion that implied that they had just extricated themselves from the monkey. It was hard to avoid the implications of the message but Professor Badger was taking no chances, so he loudly and proudly proclaimed, "Ms. Arctic, allow me to introduce you to one of our Masterpiece statues. It is called 'Holding on, letting go.'"

Arctic pondered the implications of the statue for a long time. What was she holding on to she wondered? She finally turned to the badger, whom she had decided to refer to affectionately as "The Prof," and in a thoughtful manner she said, "You know, Prof, it is not easy to figure out what we hold on to. After all, everything that makes up me seems so comfortable. It fits, like an old glove."

"You are right, Arctic. That is exactly why we call you Stuckies. Not only have you not figured out how to let go, you haven't even figured out that there is anything to let go of," Professor Badger proclaimed in a self-righteous tone, seemingly quite irritated that she was not making progress. It was quite frustrating for the more enlightened creatures not to be able to persuade the Stuckies that there was something worthy of their attention.

"Come on, let's move on. There is more to see. Let me show you some examples of how Stuckies get stuck," he said in a much more pleasant tone. Arctic willingly followed him. Stasher followed behind, checking the hallways for occasional nuts and seeds. You just never know where you are going to find food and he was not one to miss an opportunity to forage.

As they entered the next section of the museum, they walked

down a ramp and Arctic was amazed to see a small boat waiting for them at what looked like a dock. Sure enough, it was a boat with a large tiger dressed in an orange and black sailor's uniform.

He looked very dapper indeed, as he greeted them cheerfully. "Welcome aboard the good ship Enlightenment. My name is Intrepid and I will be your captain for this part of the journey," he announced.

They all jumped on board and the boat set off with their new tour guide at the helm. As the boat turned the first corner, they came to a large arch that read "Stuck World."

Wow, thought Arctic, I think I am in for the ride of my life. She was beginning to regain her sense of humor about this adventure. After all, she did not seem to be in charge of it, so why not just go along for the ride and see what happens. No point in fretting over it as no one was listening anyway.

They came to the first exhibit on their boat ride. A sign, held by a small gnome-like person said, "Entanglement Jungle." Arctic was curious. What could that mean? The boat pulled in at the dock and the captain beckoned them to get out. As they walked up the path, they saw a group of elves working in the garden, digging and singing in unison as they dug and heaved large sods of dirt over their shoulders.

It's a world of dirt and a world of hurt
It's a world of muck and a world of stuck
There's so much in the pain, and there's nothing to gain
It's a stuck world after all.

You have just one life and don't need the strife
And a chance to be free of the fettered side
Though the work it is tough, you can try hard enough
To unstuck your world after all.

As Arctic and her companions continued to walk along the path, she could hear the refrain, "It's a stuck world after all," following her along the trail. They made for a motley crew indeed, a Stucky, a squirrel, a badger and now a tiger. Who would have thought? They arrived at the first display.. There were two circles intertwined above the exhibit. Inside each circle was the image of two people sitting back to back. They looked like twins. On the ground, there were separate replicas of the two circles, but this time there were marionette dolls inside each of them. In the first circle, there were eight marionettes, all standing at attention. They were standing in groups of two, very close to each other, all facing outwards, forming a square. They looked quite rigid and unwelcoming, and it seemed clear that no one was allowed to enter their square or violate their boundaries. The looks on their faces were quite menacing, as if they were saying, "I dare you to even try to break down our defenses." As Arctic looked closer, she saw a younger doll sitting inside the square looking quite unhappy, as if she had been crying. Bursting with curiosity, Arctic could no longer contain herself and asked Professor Badger, "What does this mean? Is the girl trapped inside? Are the other dolls her guards?"

"How do you interpret it?" asked the Professor.

How annoying! Arctic was always cross when someone answered her question with another question. "I don't know," she pouted. "That's why I'm asking you and YOU are meant to be my tour guide," she exclaimed.

"Very well then, let's see," said Professor Badger with a slightly bemused tone to his voice. "I think that perhaps the young girl is trapped inside and the other dolls are preventing her from escaping."

Stasher piped up. "Not at all; that is not what I see. What I see is that they are protecting her from being hurt, as she has obviously been crying because other people have already hurt her."

"Huh! You are both wrong," said Intrepid the tiger. "It is obvious to me that she is crying because she created them in order to protect herself and now she can't work out how to get rid of them."

"Well, now I am thoroughly confused," said Arctic. "I can see that you could all be right. What is the name of this exhibit?"

"Imposing Margins," said Professor Badger.

"That is really helpful, Prof! What am I supposed to make of that?" exclaimed Arctic.

Professor Badger looked at Arctic and said, "You could decide it was about self-imposed margins and, then again, you could decide the margins were being imposed upon someone. Actually, it is entirely up to you how you interpret it. Personally, I think there can be many truths. We see what we want to see and you are focusing on the young girl inside, but what about the people doing the guarding? What might they be feeling?"

THE VILLAGE OF ILLUSIONS

Arctic reflected on the fact that Intrepid's interpretation was probably the most accurate for her. What the little girl was probably feeling was that she had built up so many defenses that she did not know how to begin to get rid of the guards. It feels like she was trapped inside the trauma of her own behaviors. Some days when she knew she was at her most defensive, she did not even like herself, and yet she seemed unable to stop the behaviors. Almost like the guards were in charge and not her.

Arctic sighed and moved on. As she walked towards the second circle, she noticed that the sign placed underneath the two circles said, "Double-trouble." She saw a house with no walls. The outside walls were all laying flat on the ground, almost as if a tornado had blown through and knocked them down and the entire floor plan was open. There were a couple of elves scurrying around, running mindlessly in and out of the house and occasionally bumping into each other. Right in the middle of the house there was another elf who was pulling on the skirt of an older elf, obviously trying to get her attention and she was trying to get away.

Arctic became quite excited. "I get it, I get it," she proclaimed. Professor Badger raised his eyebrows and Intrepid and Stasher, caught up in Arctic's enthusiasm, were jumping up and down but not really knowing why.

"It's about freedom, isn't it? They are all free to run around anywhere they want with no limits, and then there is one elf trying to hold someone back from being free," said Arctic. (She was a fast learner and she was catching on to the purpose of this museum).

"That certainly is one interpretation. Can you think of any others?" asked the Professor.

"I can," yelled Stasher before Arctic had a chance to speak. "It is not about freedom. It is about the lack of margins, or boundaries. The elves are running in and out of the house because there are no walls and therefore no systems of control. They don't know where to stop." Then, reflecting for a moment, he said, "Well, maybe it is about freedom; too much freedom."

"OK, but how does that explain the elf who is trying to stop someone from leaving?" asked Arctic.

"Oh, that's easy," said Intrepid, feeling the need to get into the conversation. "It is just another side of the same equation. Stasher is correct. The elf who is tugging at the skirt is needy and

clingy, always wanting attention. 'Joined at the hip,' I think the Stuckies of Ice Valley would call it."

"Some people have no idea of their boundaries and the result is that they go rushing around like helium balloons, not realizing the impact they are having?" added Arctic.

"Yes, and other people who have the same problem behave differently by being too needy and intruding on others' boundaries in an inappropriate manner," said the Professor.

"Can the same person be capable of both behaviors?" asked Arctic.

"I had not thought of that, but I suppose they could. It is possible that a person can behave in ways that suggest they have no sense of appropriate boundaries in their life and, at the same time, around certain people, behave in ways that aree quite needy and equally inappropriate," said Professor Badger.

"It is also possible that the house being blown down is how the person feels about their life, is it not? They once had order and control and something happened which made them feel that they no longer had control of their life," added Arctic.

"You know, Arctic, I think you are really beginning to do some gardening. Digging in your own garden is very good therapy. When you turn over the soil it becomes ready for new planting."

Arctic was not entirely clear what he was telling her, but he seemed pleased and she felt proud of herself. She was aware that there were times in her life when it felt as if she was out of control and had no boundaries around her. Then there were times when she felt insecure. On these occasions, she could become possessive and needy. Neither situation had made her feel comfortable. She was also aware that in recent years things had happened which had perhaps forever changed the landscape of her personal psyche and that the more threatened she had felt and the more hurt and rejection she experienced the more she had tightened her boundaries. She was now realizing that each incident had provided the building blocks for a high wall of defense that now felt suffocating.

It was time to move on to the next part of the tour. The small group returned to the boat and Captain Intrepid set off to their next destination. They traveled for some time without seeing any other attractions until they came across a small volcano. As they approached it, the volcano erupted. Arctic watched in amazement as the volcano was rumbling and the water they were sailing on was

THE VILLAGE OF ILLUSIONS

becoming disturbed. Captain Intrepid docked the boat alongside and beckoned everyone to get out quickly. They all hurried off to stand under a friendly palm tree, where they thought it might be safe to witness what was happening. As they watched the volcano erupt, instead of molten ash, three marionettes jettisoned from its crater onto the grass. Arctic was wide-eyed, as were Stasher and Intrepid. Professor Badger, on the other hand, looked quite composed.

The first marionette had a table tennis bat with a ball and string attached and kept hitting the ball as it constantly bounced back. The second marionette was playing with a baseball bat and a ball attached to a rope on a long pole. He kept hitting the ball, watching it wrap around the pole, then unwind to return to him. The third marionette had more freedom and flexibility. He was throwing a boomerang past the other two marionettes. It took a while, but the boomerang always returned, somehow managing to avoid hitting anyone else as it slammed back into its owner's hand. As they continued to play, the volcano rumbled quietly in the background, looking like it could erupt again at any time.

The group stood and watched this activity for some time and eventually Arctic spoke up and said, "Well, I don't know about you, but I think I need a cup of coffee before I can begin to speak about this one."

Everyone nodded in agreement. They returned to the boat, asking Intrepid to look out for a coffee shop en route. Intrepid knew the territory and quickly found them a very nice place where they could sit outside with their drinks and enjoy the view. "You first," said Stasher, indicating that Intrepid should speak.

"Not a chance. After you," said Intrepid. They both looked towards Arctic, hoping she would jump into the fray.

"I don't know where to begin," she said. "What about you Professor Badger? Can you explain that last exhibit?"

"Perhaps," said the badger, "but I would rather hear your interpretations," he said, quickly sidestepping any responsibility. After all, he was only the tour guide.

"I think it was three friends just out having fun together," said Stasher hurriedly, almost as if he was trying to convince himself of that. Sometimes he noticed that the louder he spoke the less certain he really felt about a topic, even when he was making a pronouncement about himself. For instance, when one of his squirrel friends, Miser, was asking him why he did not *share more of his stash with the other squirrels, he gave Miser a very long and loud dissertation on the value of saving for a rainy day. He was actually feeling a little defensive, as he was not sure why he did not feel inclined to share with the others. Anyway, he thought, as he shook his tail, look who is accusing whom! With a name like Miser, it felt like the nut calling the kernel black!! Now here he was again, speaking loudly, sounding convincing when he was not feeling certain.*

Fortunately, before anyone noticed, Intrepid jumped into the conversation. "Actually, I don't think they were three friends at all. They were not playing the same game and they did not seem to be paying any attention to each other. In fact, you could argue that the games they were playing were in contention with one another."

"That is interesting, Intrepid," said Arctic. "You are right. In fact, the one with the boomerang looked like he was in his own world and yet the boomerang always looked like it might come back and hit one of the others."

"Yes, and the baseball was not exactly on a short rope. What if someone had walked across its path as it was wrapping itself around that pole?" added Stasher.

"Maybe people did. We don't know, do we?" asked Intrepid.

"Well, they would have gotten hurt, that's for sure," said Stasher in a thoughtful tone.

"I think you might be on to something. What else did you see?" inquired Professor Badger.

Arctic was gaining confidence in her interpretation of these events and, in fact, was beginning to enjoy unraveling the mysteries. She enjoyed symbolism and she liked the fact that even when you thought you had answered a question or solved a puzzle, another question seemed to appear, always leaving you wondering, giving you the impression there was more work to do.

"Well, Prof, I'm beginning to think that the toys they chose to play with also have significance. They all have one thing in common," said Arctic.

Intrepid leapt to his feet and started jumping up and down, laughing as he did. "Don't be silly, Arctic, of course they don't have anything in common; a table tennis bat, a baseball and a boomerang? Girls are silly, what do they know about sports?"

Arctic became very quiet and immediately looked unsure.

THE VILLAGE OF ILLUSIONS

Perhaps Intrepid was right, what did she know about sports? After all, not only was she a girl, but she was a Stucky and a guest in their museum. They probably did know more than she did. Professor Badger waited to see if she would add anything else. When she did not he decided to change the subject.

"There is something I think you have all missed."

"What?" exclaimed Stasher and Intrepid in disbelief.

"W-e-l-l," said the Professor carefully. The way he dragged out the word "Well" made everyone know that something big was coming. "What about the volcano? How do you account for that? I think you have all been so focused on what the Marionettes were doing that you have completely forgotten how they got there." They all looked at each other and in a somewhat chastened manner Stasher spoke first.

"You're right, Professor Badger, I did forget. I think the volcano indicates the difference between work and play. Sort of Monday through Friday and then the weekend, if you know what I mean," he said laughing. "The volcano is Monday to Friday and then at the weekend you come bursting out to play."

Professor Badger laughed. "That is certainly a valid interpretation, Stasher. What about you, Arctic, what do you think?"

"I'm not sure, but I think that the volcano actually indicates something pretty traumatic or troublesome that the three marionettes have experienced and as they were thrown out of the volcano they created games to protect themselves from any more traumas."

"That is very good, Arctic," cried Intrepid.

"What were you going to say earlier, Arctic, when Intrepid laughed at you?" asked the Professor.

"Oh that! It was nothing important. I was just going to say that the thing all three had in common was that no matter how hard they tried, the ball, or the boomerang always bounced back to them."

Everyone's eyes fixated on her.

"What?"

"That is it, Arctic. That is precisely IT," said Stasher. "Something bad happened to them and in an effort to cope, they developed patterns of behavior. The problem is that the patterns of behavior, which may have served them well at the time, continue to repeat themselves and always seem to bring the same result back to them. Sort of like their worst fear kept being thrown back in their face. Isn't that right, Professor?"

"Yes, almost as if the thing they most fear is the thing they keep drawing back to themselves. So if you fear being rejected you set yourself up to be rejected." added Intrepid.

"I think you might be right, Stasher. We can never really know, but I think it is a very plausible explanation," said Professor Badger.

"Gosh, I'm exhausted. Where do we go from here?"asked Arctic. "I realize now why you call me a Stucky and I realize that this is the Stucky Museum, but are there any lighthearted ways in which Stuckies get stuck?"

Everyone laughed at the contradiction and Professor Badger motioned that it was time to move on.

Arctic was reflecting on Stasher's interpretation of the Marionettes and realizing that she had most certainly created situations in her life where the same patterns of behavior kept repeating themselves. It was frustrating because she kept thinking she had solved something, only to discover that she had found new and creative ways to manifest the same negative patterns and tendencies.

As they walked back to their boat Artic said, "Oh, by the way, what was the name of that exhibit?"

"5R Volcano," Professor Badger informed her.

"5R Volcano, what do the 5 R's stand for?"

"Well, I could make you think about it, but I reckon by this time you should be seeing the pattern, so I will make it easy for you. They are Rejection, Resentment, Restimulation, Reiteration and Reverberation," said the Professor.

The Lowland Games:

The five R's certainly gave Arctic even more to think about. What were her issues of rejection and resentment and in what ways did she become restimulated by past events and reiterate old behaviors? Did she understand the reverberations of her behaviors on herself and others? Much to ponder on and certainly many questions were reverberating in her head.

In the meantime, the group was on the move. They all made their way back to the boat and Intrepid guided them safely out of the waterway and back to dry land.

It had been quite an experience. In what ways could all of the things she had learned apply to her life? What could she do

THE VILLAGE OF ILLUSIONS

differently? As she was walking and reflecting on these issues, they came across a large field where a group of people had gathered to watch some games. Oh no, just when she thought they were finished, here they went again!

As if he had read her mind, Professor Badger said, "Come on, Arctic, let's go and watch the games."

As they walked across the field, they saw a large sign across the entranceway that said, "Welcome to the Ice Valley Lowland Games." It looked like a Village Fair. There were stalls where people were selling memorabilia and in the main display area, there were a number of games going on simultaneously. At the far end of the park, there was an outdoor theater and stage and they could hear strange music in the distance. They walked towards the stalls to explore what the vendors were selling or displaying. The first stall they came to was the Heritage Hut. *What is my heritage?* Arctic wondered. "Find your Clan and your Tartan," the sign proudly proclaimed.

Arctic turned to her friends. "That would be fun to have your own tartan. Help me pick one. They all look so beautiful."

Stasher jumped up onto the counter first, checking out each sample of tartan. Intrepid stepped forward and picked up a couple of samples. "This is a nice one, Arctic. What about this one?"

Professor Badger was not quite so fast to action. He was standing back from the others, wearing one of his most questioning looks.

"Not so fast, my friends," he said in a tone that was soft, but undeniably authoritative. "You cannot just pick a tartan. You have to know who you are, where you came from and then you can determine your Clan. Not everyone is entitled to wear the tartan."

Arctic looked concerned. "Oh! Then I think I might have a problem," she said. "I don't remember where I came from, or the name of my family of origin, and quite honestly, I'm not very sure what my real name is now. All I know is that people call me Arctic of Ice Valley." Arctic looked very sad, sadder in fact than she had looked at the beginning of this journey when she met the anonymous snowman. It was one thing to live with the oblivion of Ice Valley, it was quite another to realize that you might have had a past and memories that held the promise of something more warming than Ice Valley. Intrepid and Stasher also looked sad. They felt powerless. How could they help their new friend?

Helen Turnbull, Ph. D.

As always, Professor Badger had an answer. "I"ll tell you what, Arctic. Let us not worry about the tartan. Let us move on and see what else we can discover and perhaps we can find your identity along the way. We can come back for the tartan if we find more information."

The next stall they came to was entitled "Memories" and as Arctic approached it she realized that many of the pictures, which were in smart antique frames, looked like pictures of her when she was much younger. She looked at them in amazement and memories came flooding in. She remembered the laughter, the outfits she wore, the freedom she used to feel. She picked up a picture of herself standing at the bow of a very large ferry, sailing across a wide river. There were seagulls following the ship and she could see land off in the distance. She did not know where it was but she knew it was a place where she had felt safe and happy. She smiled as she remembered those days. They were carefree days, days when the only worry she had was what she was having for dinner or what she needed to wear that day and how quickly she could eat so that she could get back to walking on the shore. She was beginning to realize that there had been a warmer life before Ice Valley and she was staring at the evidence almost as if she could reach out and touch it. She gently ran her fingers across the photograph, conjuring up memories of a time gone by when she used to enjoy the feel of the sea breeze in her hair, the wind in her face and the sense of freedom she got from being out of doors. Maybe she could rediscover her sweetness after all.

Intrepid pulled at her coat and beckoned her to follow him to the next stall. He was hungry and had settled his eyes on a veritable feast of ethnic delights. Arctic laughed as her eyes delighted in the array of foods that seemed very familiar to her. It is a strange thing how the power of food can immediately reconnect us to other memories. The combination of savory and sweet offerings reminded her of times past and a distant land. At the back of the stall, there were piping hot meat pastries. She recalled an image of walking along the promenade with her family eating hot pastries on a cold windy day. They were a nice family, always laughing together and having fun. Then there were the chocolate bars and the candies. She succumbed to the temptation to purchase one. She mused on the power of comfort food from the past. Even though she knew it was no longer healthy to eat these items, the compensatory sensation of doing so was almost *like eating fruit from the trees of stability.*

She wandered to the next stall, where she found lots of trinkets, paperweights and brooches. They also seemed vaguely familiar and she picked up a silver pin, which the stall owner described to her as a Celtic cross. Just looking at it made her feel connected to the earth in a way she had seldom experienced. She purchased the pin and ceremoniously put it on her jacket, feeling somehow that she was reclaiming part of her heritage.

In the distance, she could hear music. It was haunting music and seemed to be calling to her. She started walking across the field in the direction of the music and her three friends followed her. On the way, they had to pass a roped-off section of the field where there were groups of men engaged in some sort of sports activities. One man was attempting to pick up a very large pole. He stumbled a few times, but eventually he picked it up with both hands, ran down the field clutching the pole and threw it as far as he could. All of the spectators applauded, but the man looked quite dejected. Arctic was curious.

"Why would anyone want to pick up such a large pole and what would possess them to run anywhere with it, far less trying to throw it?" she asked.

"Oh, that is a Habit Pole and people are trying to toss it in such a way that it goes over on its own length. If they are successful, they get points towards breaking a habit. They need twenty-one points in order to completely break the habit and as they only acquire three points with each successful tossing of the Habit Pole, they need to be able to throw it seven times," Professor Badger explained.

Arctic wondered what habits she needed to break but found the idea of tossing such a large pole to be quite daunting..

"That seems quite extreme, Professor. Is there any other way to break a habit, which might take less energy?" Arctic asked.

"Yes, there is, but I am not sure if it is really any easier. It takes twenty-one days to form a new habit, so if you can stop doing something for twenty-one days and replace it with something better, then you have a good chance of being successful. Twenty-one days will feel like a big commitment, but the effort will most likely be worth it," said the Professor.

"Why do all the poles look like they have notches and nail holes in them?" asked Stasher who had been standing a safe distance from the pole tossing.

"Good question, Stasher," said the Professor. "That is because every time a person indulges in a bad habit a nail is hammered into the pole and each time they successfully avoid that bad habit, a nail is taken out. However, as you will see, even when the habit is broken the nail holes leave evidence of damage."

This was feeling a little depressing, so Arctic walked quickly towards the music. When she got to the other side of the field, she found a group of men playing very haunting, almost mystical music. She asked a man close by next to explain the music to her. He looked at her strangely and told her, "It is the Pipes and Drums, of course."

As she stood there entranced, listening to the Pipes and Drums she turned to Stasher and Intrepid who were standing close by.

"You know, the sound from that music stirs my blood, but I am not sure why. Sometimes I feel like a stranger in a strange land. It feels as if my soul has lived with this music for a very long time," she said, her voice trailing off as the music nearly drowned out her next words. "I don't think I have quite discovered my heritage, Professor, but I feel closer to who I used to be than I did earlier today."

The Professor looked fondly at Arctic. "I think you have made incredible progress, Arctic. Ice Valley was not built in a day and rediscovering your former self and your heritage is not a 24-hour event. You did not get yourself stuck overnight and becoming unstuck is quite a lengthy process. I think you will be working on this for quite some time. Unraveling the complex threads we weave is a lifetime of work.

"Perhaps you can come back here next year and by that time you will be able to claim one of these tartans as your own."

"I would like that," said Arctic, "but what do you mean that I have to keep working on it?"

"Let's sit down over here," said Professor Badger, indicating a park bench, "and we will talk about some of the things you have experienced today."

Arctic was not sure she had the energy left to summarize such a momentous day, but she complied, knowing in her heart that this was an important conversation. It was really quite an honor, she reflected, to have Professor Badger spend so much time on her and she felt very validated and worthy at that moment. Intrepid and Stasher seated themselves at Arctic's and Professor Badger's feet and put on their best listening ears. Everyone waited.

Professor Badger cleared his throat. "This has been quite a day for you, Arctic. I think it might help if we spend some time reflecting on what you have seen and learned and how you are now feeling."

Artic took a deep breath and began to speak. "Truthfully, Professor Badger, I am feeling quite tired and overwhelmed, but in a good way. I think I know that today was a very meaningful journey for me and yet it has all been so much that it feels like I have packed a year of learning into one day. If I had to capture in a few words what all of that has been about, I would have to say 'reflection and awareness.' I have had a chance to reflect on many aspects of my life and become more aware of some things, which perhaps have been keeping me stuck. I know we can spend a lifetime unfolding and moving towards wholeness, differentiating ourselves from others."

"Are there any specifics that you feel you have learned which you can use as building blocks to keep you on the path?" asked the Professor.

"Yes, I believe there are. Let me see.... I believe I more fully understand that the little girl inside of me has been hurting for quite some time and that I have major issues of rejection that I need to work on. I also believe that that has caused me to mismanage my boundaries on occasions. Sometimes I am too expansive and needy and other times I have built walls and barriers around myself that serve to keep people out. I can be rude and defensive with people. I have developed some bad habits as a result and I do not always like myself. I think all of these defenses have caused me to lose my sweetness and my sense of myself as a good person. I think just like tossing the habit pole, that I would like to rediscover the real me. I have quite a lot of work ahead of me. I guess the good news is that I still seem capable of presenting a positive face to the world at large and it is really only me and the people who are close to me who see my real vulnerabilities."

Everyone nodded in agreement, feeling that Arctic had done an exceptional job of summarizing her day.

"You know, Arctic, it has been a very long day and it is time to take you home. We will walk back with you to the path that leads to Ice Valley. The least we can do is see you safely home, and we'd like to spend a few more minutes with you," said Intrepid, trying to sound calmer than he felt. He had grown fond of Arctic and was not accustomed to showing his emotions.

The three friends had grown very fond of Arctic during this journey of discovery. They now felt like part of her family.

As they walked past the Tree of Rejection, Arctic stopped for another look. She saw beautiful frosted icicle decorations hanging from the branches. One of them looked like a delicately woven crystal sphere.

As she stared at it she said, "You know, I think I began my life as a sunflower and somehow have ended up as an icicle. I am not sure what happened."

The three friends looked thoughtful. As always, Professor Badger poured forth his wisdom.

"Arctic, you might be right, but that icicle is very beautiful and you could try thinking of it as a very delicate and precious piece of crystal."

"I am not sure you can ever become a sunflower again," added Intrepid, "but you could do what Professor Badger is suggesting and work on turning the icicle into something much more precious. Icicles do melt, you know, but crystal is very strong and very intriguing, not to mention the fact that precious gems are very beautiful.

"You can build yourself a crystal palace instead of an ice hut, and by listening to your inner wisdom you might be able to add some amethyst to your collection," added Stasher, not wanting to be left out of this very important conversation.

"Stasher, meeting you today has been an incredible gift and I thank you. Are you now free to return to the life you once led?" asked Arctic.

"Oh, thank you for asking, Arctic. Yes, I am now free, but not to return to my previous life. Like you, I intend to return to a better life and although I will continue to forage and stash I will do so mindful of how I can help others. Thank you for rescuing me and for sharing this piece of your personal journey with me," said Stasher with tears in his eyes.

Professor Badger cleared his throat as the others lined up beside him on the path. "We have a gift for you, Arctic. We have thought long and hard about this gift as we wanted to give you something that would help you in the future and perhaps prevent you from getting stuck again." He snapped his fingers and, much to Arctic's amazement, a brown twig broomstick danced onto the pathway in front of her, sweeping the snow and ice as it danced. It seemed like a very cheerful broom.

THE VILLAGE OF ILLUSIONS

"Allow me to introduce you to your new companion," said Professor Badger proudly. "This is Cinnamon Broom. Cinnamon has healing power, spirituality, success and the power to protect. (Cunningham 1996, p.75). Her job is to sweep the path before you in order that you will have minimal obstructions." The friends all applauded and if anyone was looking closely, they could have seen a tear trickle down each of their faces.

Arctic was overwhelmed with their thoughtful gift. She had such low self esteem that she was often amazed when she discovered how much people cared for her.

"Hello, Cinnamon, it is very nice to meet you. I am sure we are going to become very good friends," said Arctic with a smile.

As Arctic walked away from her friends, she felt sad at leaving them. She had found a surprising amount of comfort being with them, despite not knowing them for very long. She knew they cared enough to work through these issues with her. At the same time, she was excited about new prospects. Carving a future that was not so dependent on barriers, blockades and ice was very exciting. What could it look like? It already felt lighter, more fun, and most definitely less cold. As she continued to walk down the path home, she noticed that the ice was beginning to melt all around her. Snowdrops and Crocus flowers were appearing through the snow on little tufts of grass. It seemed to her that the cold winter of Ice Valley was ending and spring was appearing, with all of its potential. She wondered how the anonymous snowman, who so carefully guarded the tree of rejection, would survive without the frost. Then again, she intuitively knew if spring flowers were to bloom around that tree, that her snowman could find a new job as a beautiful pond, full of life-giving oxygen at the bottom of the garden. She would come for walks, enjoy the pond and perhaps visit her friends who lived around it.

Amethyst sighed as she put the wise silver needle back in her pocket, closed the book and returned it to its rightful place on the shelf. As she secured the secret door to the tree and returned the anchor, she thought about the myriad of stories cataloged in the oak tree libraries. Arctic's story was one of her personal favorites, but she knew of many others, which she would visit another day.

When she returned to the oak bench, Patience was sitting waiting for her, looking pensive..

Helen Turnbull, Ph. D.

"What is going through your mind, Patience? I can almost hear the wheels turning."

"I think I am just beginning to fully realize that all of the people in the stories, including you, Amethyst, are really parts of me. The issues, challenges and dilemmas are also mine and it is up to me what I do with them. You play a very special role in helping me to look at myself and I need to listen to you more often. There is a Princess living inside of me. Funny thing is that I have always wanted to be a Princess. All this time I didn't know." Patience smiled.

As Amethyst and Patience walked back up the avenue, they saw someone waving to them from the steps of Crystal Palace. It was a very charming, golden teddy bear, dressed in full Highland Dress. The two women laughed and waved as they recognized the essence of their outer self, looking happy, adorable, soft, and cuddly and delightfully Scottish. The bear emanated such a positive energy and generosity of spirit that just being in her company filled everyone around with warmth and good feelings. As they walked towards her, Amethyst invited Patience to join her and was looking forward to an evening of fun and good conversation, with perhaps some Celtic music in the background.

SCOTTISH TEDDY BEAR

Chapter Ten
The Island State of Inner Wisdom

> *"It may be objected that such an inquiry concerns no one but myself. Not so: if any individual – a Pepys or a Rousseau, an exceptional or a run-of the mill character, reveals (herself) honestly, everyone, more or less, becomes involved. It is impossible for (her) to shed light on (her) own life without at some point illuminating the lives of others."*
> *(Beauvoir 1952)*

As the two women walked, Patience began to ask questions.

"Why do people come here? What do they get out of it?"

"The search to understand oneself is arguably the most important journey a person could take in their lifetime. The question 'who am I?' resonates inside all of us. People expend a lot of energy, time and money looking for answers outside of themselves, but actually the answers are to be found inside and not outside. There is no point in expecting others to make us happy, or blaming others for our problems if we are not happy ourselves, and are not willing to take responsibility for our own actions."

"It does not sound too easy," said Patience.

"No, I guess not. Although the rewards are significant and life changing, the journey can be long and arduous and requires commitment and tenacity."

AMETHYST & CRYSTAL PALACE

THE VILLAGE OF ILLUSIONS

"Why are you called Amethyst?" asked Patience, suddenly curious to know..

"When I was a young princess, my mother told me that I was called Amethyst because the color of amethyst is very important in the color spectrum. It has spiritual qualities and can guide people towards deeper understanding."

The inner calm initiated by amethysts enables people to "let go and trust," to surrender and see beyond the daily cycles and circumstances which seem to weigh us down. (Raphaell 1985, p. 79-80).

"Do you like it when people come here?" asked Patience. "After all, this is your home and maybe having so many visitors feels intrusive. A bit like living in a holiday town and getting tired of the snowbirds."

"I am delighted to have visitors. I know that when people arrive here they have traveled far and worked hard to justify their trip. A trip to the Island State means that that individual has come to the realization that they need to explore their own attitudes and behaviors and it is time for them to change and cast aside outmoded ways."

Helen Turnbull, Ph. D.

STORY TIME

THE VILLAGE OF ILLUSIONS

Patience and Amethyst came to the pond, where the birds and the turtles, oblivious to their presence, were deep in conversation.

"You know only too well, Mrs. Blue Jay, that that is not how people operate. It seems there is too much conflict and even hatred," said Octogenarian.

"Where do you start if you want to change that?" asked Flapper.

"Oh, it is quite simple, actually," said Octogenarian, hesitating only for a second. "Well, on reflection, maybe it is not so simple. You have to start with yourself. The answers are inside. You have to be conscious of the choices you make. You have to be aware how your behavior affects others. That is not always as easy as it seems. For example, people who send mixed messages, friends who are friendly one day and then behave in unfriendly, inconsistent ways another day, are not always conscious of how their behavior is confusing and hurtful to others. People talk about disliking gossips and then gossip themselves, or people ask how you are doing and then talk about how they are doing. These people rarely see the impact of their behavior on others, or stop to realize that perhaps they need to change."

"Huh! If they were a friend, you would think they would always be friendly. How hard can that be?" asked Mrs. Blue Jay. "It would seem simpler to look inside first; there is less distance to travel."

"Ah, yes, but that is not what people do. They usually find it more comfortable to focus their energies on others. After all, who wants to blame themselves for their shortcomings? Amethyst provides them with a safe space and an inner sanctum for self-exploration but they don't always listen or take advantage of it. When they do, the results are spectacular. I am proud to be part of Amethyst's team, helping people to grow and develop and to realize that there is more than one perspective to a story," said Octogenarian, pushing his head as far out of his shell as it would go and almost standing to attention as he spoke. The others nodded in agreement. The animals looked up and for the first time, realized that Patience and Amethyst had been listening.

Amethyst laughed, "Thanks, everyone needs to feel appreciated. I am glad you are all part of the team also."

They were approaching the stairs to the Palace when Patience exclaimed, "Wow! Look at that clock tower. It's beautiful."

"The clock face is made of rose quartz and amethyst crystals. The clock itself has beautiful chimes. They do not chime every hour, but chime instead when someone gains an insight that enlightens them and enables them to move forward. The melodic tone of the chimes makes my spirits soar. Some weeks they chime a lot and other weeks it is very quiet. People sometimes refer to them as 'Amethyst's bells' but the bells are actually chiming for them and ringing in a new direction for their life work. I feel honored to be a part of that, but just like with you, Patience, I cannot do their work for them; they have to do that."

Patience grimaced. "I think I know what you mean, Amethyst."

"Here we are," announced Amethyst as the two women arrived at the top of the stairs and walked towards a very comfortable looking living room with sumptuous lounge chairs.

"Before we have dinner, let's have a seat and talk for a while about your experiences this evening."

Patience sank into one of the chairs, groaning as she did. "Oh, Amethyst, do I really have to look at this stuff? I was having such a good time. Now you want me to make sense of it!"

"Remember what I told you about the unexamined life, Patience. I know it is not always easy to look at our own "stuff" as you call it, but that really is the only way you can make progress."

"Oh, all right then! Procrastination is my middle name and I would much rather put this off till another night, or even another dream, but if you insist. Where do I begin?"

"Well what do you think you have learned from all of these stories this evening? We can look at them one at a time, we can talk about the people in the stories, or we can just have a general discussion about what impact they all had on you," said Amethyst.

"Maybe a little bit of everything really. I am feeling overwhelmed right now, but the one thing that really sinks in with me is that all of the different characters in the stories are all parts of me. I can identify with every single person and can recognize parts of myself, even Joe K. Fixit, because I can be a bit pushy, too. I saw pieces of myself in all of them. That is pretty sobering, is it not?"

Amethyst was silent and after a short pause for breath, Patience continued.

"At the beginning of each story I kind of thought I knew the people, recognized them as playing the part of someone I know in my real life, and then eventually it would sink in that the traits they were displaying were actually my characteristics. I once heard that what we like in others is a reflection of ourselves and what we don't like in others is similarly that which we do not like about ourselves.. I don't really know if that is true, but after bearing witness to all the villagers and their adventures I realize that I am them and they are me. Now, what I should do with that knowledge I am not sure. What do you think, Amethyst?""Which character stands out most for you?"

Patience thought for a few minutes. "Arctic of Ice Valley, without question. Her story speaks so strongly to my own feelings and experience. I have always had issues with rejection. I work so hard to be liked. I hate being rejected and I let people treat me in ways I don't deserve just because I don't want them to be angry at me, or dislike me.

Over the years I have become angry at the way I have been treated and I fear it has made me hard. I used to think of myself as a nice person, a sweet person, and now I feel as if I have developed such a thick skin, a tough exterior, that no one could get close to me. Even I don't like myself some days. So, yes, Arctic definitely resonates with me. It would be nice to find ways to let my own ice melt a little. People hurt me and then in return I hurt them or sometimes just take my anger out on other people. It makes no sense to hurt people you love and yet so often that is what we do."

"Which stories reminded you of the people who have hurt you?"

"Yikes, Amethyst. You don't give up do you? Actually, probably all of them do in a way, because we make up stories in our heads about the way things are and what we think people have done to us. Not all of it is true, it is just our perception, maybe our way of making ourselves the victim in the story, a kind of 'poor me' scenario. I think there is the story and then there is what really happened, but no one has the "true version" of what really happened. We all have our own unique twist on it, but to answer your question more directly, I suppose that Joe K. Fixit reminds me of the difficult relationships I have had with the men in my life and how being oppressed by them has in some ways resulted in my being both emotionally injured, and also in my intimidating other people in return. That is why I feel like I have lost my sweetness, I suppose.

The Nomadic Ms. Cosmopolitan definitely reminds me of myself as I struggle with self-esteem issues, eating for comfort and weight gain. Her relationships with her friends made me smile as I have many friends like that, but also I have many pieces of myself that remind me of my friends, good and bad."

Patience paused to catch her breath and Amethyst waited silently for her next response.

"Mrs. Baker's Dilemma was an interesting story, particularly as it made me think about all of the different emotional states I get stuck in on a regular basis. I really resonated with her being stuck in the State of Anxiety. I think I live there quite a lot and it is a very tiring state indeed. You know the awful thing about being stuck in these negative places is that when I am there, I am totally convinced that that is reality, almost as if the situation has more power over me than it deserves. In that moment

I cannot imagine that any one else's version of the same incident can have as much significance as mine. I can be the ultimate drama queen and while my life is never dull, it does not always need to be filled with so much drama. I am sure if I tried, I could learn to be more pragmatic about things and not turn everything into Opening night at the Opera."

"You have mentioned Mrs. Baker, Joe K. Fixit and Ms. Cosmopolitan, but what about the Lost Brother and the Queen of Illusions?" asked Amethyst.

"Ah, I figured you were not going to let me ignore these stories. Although they were among the first stories I experienced, I guess I left them for last."

"Yes, I noticed that also. Is that significant do you think?"

"Not sure. It might be," responded Patience. "The Lost Brother story makes me think about a lot of things, particularly around my desire to influence people I care about on the way they run their lives, or at least my need for them to live their lives differently. My brother is someone very like the brother in the story and I could identify strongly with Victoria. I love my brother, but he marches to a different drum from mine. I used to think we were close, but we have grown apart over the years and it has not always been easy to watch what has been happening to him. In recent years we have been trying to reconnect, but so much has happened and we live very different lives now. It is sad how people who love each other just drift apart." Her voice trailed off to a whisper as her reflections continued.

"I realized many years ago that I could not live his life for him, but I do feel an enormous sense of loss that he has not been available to me all these years."

"Do you think there is a connection between this and your sense of being rejected?" asked Amethyst.

"I don't think so. I don't feel rejected by my brother…..but perhaps I do feel some issues of abandonment. I am not angry about it, I am just sad at the loss."

"What did you learn from the Lost Brother story?"

"Oh, I think perhaps it is important to realize that you cannot control other people and you have to walk on your own path to the beat of your own drum. In addition, I think maybe I should appreciate the time I do spend with people I love. It is more fragile than I realize. When you grow up together you just assume you have forever and then you look around and time has passed and what do you have?"

"And the Queen of Illusions?" asked Amethyst.

"Oh well, no prizes for guessing, Amethyst, that that story speaks to me of my parents. I have not had the easiest relationship with my mother over the years. I wish she had been able to do more with her life. I know that she did not have the nicest of childhoods and I understand that. My father also died when I was young and I think I am quite angry about being left to cope with life on my own. I have been very successful at many things, but not in my significant relationships, with my family and significant partners.

"Do you feel you are worthy of being loved?"

"No, I don't think I do," said Patience, sounding like she had surprised herself with her answer. "Intellectually I know that I am, but when you ask me that question I know in my soul that I don't believe that I am and I don't really know why."

"Do you know what might have happened to make you feel like that?" asked Amethyst.

"Phew! I wish I did, and then I could overcome it. Perhaps I feel like I have failed because I can't relate to my mother, or because my brother and I are not close, or even because Dad died and we could not hold the family together. I really don't know. I also know that in my relationships with men I have tried too hard to be loved and it seemed the harder I tried the less I succeeded. I guess all these these failures lead up to my concluding that I don't deserve to be loved," said Patience.

"Do you expect to be rejected?"

"Yes, I believe at either a conscious or subconscious level I go into most situations anticipating rejection. When it doesn't happen I am even capable of making up a story about why they should have rejected me."

"Do you have any idea why you feel so badly about yourself?"

"Not exactly. I think I am a nice person, a good person, an intelligent person, but my self worth does not seem very high. I have been thinking about the fact that I felt abandoned by my father when he died, and I am wondering if there is any connection between that and my feelings of rejection.

"One of the things I have noticed from all of these stories, Amethyst, is that there is a difference between the way life is and the way we wish it could be. We make up stories in our heads all of the time. Some of the stories are about the way we wish life was and there is nothing wrong with dreaming I guess. The other stories are the ones we create to justify what has happened to us. It seems to me that there is what happened and then there is the story you make up about what happened. Actually, there are probably multiple stories about what happened as everyone involved will have their own version."

"So, what are you saying, Patience?"

"I think I am saying that there is no such thing as reality, it is all just an illusion. We all make up our own versions of reality and then we live out of what is in our heads."

"Then a piece of what I hear you saying is that we need to be careful what we fill our heads with?"

"Yes, I believe so. I have a propensity to be very emotional and dramatic about everything and the story takes on a life of its own. I also tend to look for the negatives and maybe I need to be more positive."

"That is a good start, Patience, but it is more than that. If, as you acknowledge, the stories in your head are driving your life, then you also need to be able to trust your inner wisdom and listen to your inner voice. You need to be able to see without your eyes. It is almost irrelevant who caused you to do what. The real issue is what are you going to do to create your own reality. Blaming others is a waste of your energy. Stay focused on moving forward. You are faced in life with many roads to follow, many forks in the road. You cannot know what stories will unfold until you choose the road. Some roads will lead to contentment, joy and happiness, and others to pain and sorrow. Regardless of the roads you choose you cannot change what's over, only where you go from here. Yesterday is gone, tomorrow is not here and the only moment you can experience is now. You life's work, Patience, is to know yourself. You will travel far, but it's a long journey to find out who you are."

"Wow, Amethyst, that is quite a speech. I am humbled at the thought. I suspect tonight's dream is just the tip of the iceberg in finding out who I am."

"Yes, Patience, I'm sure you are right. We will leave the rest of the story to unfold in other dreams."

"Food for thought," said Patience

"Speaking of which, let's eat, shall we? " said Amethyst.

Having spent a quite delightful few hours having dinner and friendly conversation at the Palace, it was time for the evening to end.

"Well, Patience, we have come to the end of our journey together and it is time for you to return home," said Amethyst

Patience looked askance at Amethyst. She was not ready to leave. "Will I ever see you again?" she asked anxiously.

"When you are ready Patience, we will meet again, but in the meantime just know that I am with you always; you only have to listen to your inner voice, or watch for my messengers, the morning doves, the turtles and the butterflies."

With that, Amethyst bent down, picked up a handful of the gold dust on the path and sprinkled it over Patience. "Remember Patience, you are already a Princess."

Patience woke up the next morning feeling surprisingly refreshed. She was now ready to write that letter she had promised her sister for her niece. While she was at it, she might even make a list for herself. As she stepped out of bed, she noticed something on the floor. She bent down to pick it up and it was a handful of golden threads. She smiled as she remembered asking Amethyst if she could take some of the threads home. She carefully put them on her writing desk, promising herself that the threads would be a constant reminder of her dream and her commitment to weave new patterns for herself. She would continue to work to free herself from her own baggage.

In the meantime, back at the Village of Illusions, Mrs. Baker had rented a stall at the Village Square and was enthusiastically selling tickets for tours to the Island State of Inner Wisdom. "Come one, come all – take the journey of a lifetime," she called to every passerby.

Chapter Eleven
Reflections

Patience sat down at her writing desk and took out her best paper and fountain pen. She thought for a few moments, reached her hand out to touch the golden threads on her desk and then began to write.

Dear Caledonia:

A few days ago, your mother asked me if I would write to you and let you know how much you mean to me. She also asked me to share some of my life lessons and wisdom with you. I have been giving that some considerable thought. I had an amazing dream last night and I will let the stories from my dream speak for themselves.

As you know, I love to play golf, and I have heard it suggested that the most challenging distance in golf is the distance between your ears. The biggest struggle people have with golf is not physical skill, but what is going on in their heads. I have always believed that the game of golf mirrors the game of life just as the power of my mind and thoughts is a central driving force in how I conduct myself. My attitude to life, my self-confidence and self-talk are major factors that significantly influence the outcome.

Things happen; life has a way of intervening. I have concluded that much of my discomfort over the years has come, not from what has happened to me, but from what I did with the information or situation. The distance between my ears was always the longest road to haul. It was my attitude that managed my mouth. How I constructed my reality had everything to do with the outcome. Had I used my emotional energies differently I could have accomplished so much more, been so much more productive.

Anyone who knows me would say I have been successful and yet, despite this, I have spent years worrying about pleasing others and not always pleasing myself. I have often mediated between my best self and my worst self. I have strived to be liked while not always liking myself. I have spent many hours feeling anxious about relationships. I have been hurt by what I perceived to be rejection from others. I have not always recognized that my perception was not their reality. In the face of evidence to the contrary, I have felt insecure and not believed in myself. I have let others try to control me, while at the same time trying to control others. I have tried to live the life others wanted for me and I have tried to have others live the life I wanted for them. I have sought my happiness through others while forgetting to see myself. Perhaps most of all, I have learned that the more tightly I held on and defended myself the further away from happiness I moved. If I could wind the clock back I would spend less energy working on the wrong things and the wrong people and much more energy taking my life in positive directions. I would spend my 86,400 seconds per day more wisely.

I have learned that it is important to fill my head with positive self-talk, just as it is important to listen to the guidance from my inner voice. If I follow my intuition, it will steer me in the right direction. If I believe in myself, others will join me. If I sound insecure, I will make people insecure about me. If I believe I can achieve great things, then I will. If I have passion for what I do, then all things are possible. I read a car bumper sticker recently that said, "Those who do not follow their dreams will try to destroy yours." Do not let others define your passion or destroy your enthusiasm for life.

I have watched you grow and develop into an outstanding young adult. You are a beautiful person. You are kind and sensitive to your family and friends and often seem wise and thoughtful, sometimes beyond your years. Your eyes, ears and heart are always open and you seem to use them judiciously.

Continue to walk your own path and always be respectful of the woman in the glass. Pooh Bear expressed the thought that if you cannot find your shoes you should remember where you last left your feet. (Hoff 1982) I believe that is very good advice. I would add, that if you cannot find your Self you should remember where you last left your energy. Pay attention to the stories you create in your head, listen to your inner wisdom. Direct your energies wisely, weave straw into gold and strive to achieve your greatest potential.

Love and hugs,
Your adoring Aunt Patience

The Woman in the Glass

When you get what you want in your struggle for self
And the world makes you queen for a day,
Just go to the mirror and look at yourself,
And see what that woman has to say.
For it isn't your father or mother or husband
Whose judgment upon you must pass;
The person whose verdict counts most in your life
Is the one staring back from the glass.
She's the person to please, never mind all the rest,
For she's with you clear up to the end.
And you've passed your most dangerous, difficult test
If the woman in the glass is your friend.
You may fool the whole world down the pathway of life,
And get pats on your back as you pass.
But your final reward will be heartache and tears
If you've cheated the woman in the glass.

(Author unknown)
(StoryBin.com 2000)

You and Yourself

It is rewarding to find someone whom you like, but it is essential to like yourself.

It is heartening to recognize someone as a good and decent human being, but it is indispensable to view yourself as acceptable.

It is a delight to discover people who are worthy of respect, admiration and love, but it is vital to believe yourself deserving of these things.

For you cannot live in someone else. You cannot find yourself in someone else. You cannot be given a life by someone else. Of all the people you will know in a lifetime, you are the only one you will never leave or lose.

To the question of your life, you are the only answer. To the problems of your life, you are the only solution.

(Author Unknown)
(StoryBin.com 2000)

References

Anderson, W. T. (1997). The Future of the Self : Exploring the Post-Identity society. New York, NY, Penguin Putnam Inc.

Andrews, T. (2001). Animal Speak : The Spiritual & Magical Powers of Creatures Great and Small. St. Paul, Minn., Llewllyn Publishers.

Aronson, E. (1999). The Social Animal. New York, N.Y., Worth Publishers.

Beauvoir, S. d. (1952). America day by day. London, Gerald Duckworth.

Bentz, V. M. (1989). Becoming Mature: Childhood Ghosts and Spirits. Hawthorne, N.Y., Aldine De Gruyter Inc.

Carroll, L. (1960). Alice's Adventures in Wonderland and Through the Looking Glass. New York, NY, Signet Classic, Penguin Books Ltd.

Cunningham, S. (1996). Cunningham's Encyclopedia of Magical Herbs. St. Paul, Minnesota, Llewellyn Publications.

Hoff, B. (1982). The Tao of Pooh. London, Penguin Books.

O'Connor, J. and I. McDermott (1997). The Art of Systems Thinking. Hammersmith, London, Harper Collins Inc.

O'Keefe, C. (1990). The Hummingbird. Dallas, Texas, Leadership America.

Photiou, T. (2001). Inspirational Thoughts. Middlesex, England, Ocean Books.

Raphaell, K. (1985). Crystal Enlightenment. Santa Fe, New Mexico, Aurora Press.

Silbey, U. (1987). The Complete Crystal Guidebook. San Rafael, California, U-Read Publications Inc.

StoryBin.com (2000). The Woman in the Glass.

StoryBin.com (2000). You and Yourself.

Thondup, T. (1998). The Healing Power of Mind. Boston, Shambhala.

www.rhymes.org.uk (2003). Jack Spratt, www.rhymes.org.uk. Unknown.

Printed in the United States
40446LVS00005B/262-360